HOW CREATIVE
ARE YOU?

How Creative Are You?

Eugene Raudsepp

A PERIGEE BOOK

Perigee Books
are Published by
G. P. Putnam's Sons
200 Madison Avenue
New York, N.Y. 10016

Library of Congress Cataloging in Publication Data

Raudsepp, Eugene.
How creative are you?

1. Creative ability—Testing.   I.   Title.
BF408.R2425   1981   153.3'5'0287   80-39812
ISBN 0-399-50513-X

First Perigee Printing, 1981

Designed by Bernard Schleifer

Printed in the United States of America

2   3   4   5   6   7   8   9

ACKNOWLEDGMENTS

WHILE IT IS well-nigh impossible to recall the names of all those people to whom one is indebted, a few come to mind. Particularly relevant have been the researches and contributions of J. P. Guilford, Sidney J. Parnes, Alex F. Osborn, Donald W. MacKinnon, Gary A. Davis, William E. Herrmann, Dudley Lynch, William J. J. Gordon and George M. Prince.

I am most especially indebted to Ross L. Mooney and Calvin W. Taylor for their pioneering work and validation of the inventory approach to the assessment of creative ability. I also wish to express my gratitude to my friend and colleague Joseph C. Yeager for his unfailing good advice and generous assistance. Much of his thinking and keen observations permeate Part V of this book, Creativity at Work: The Politics of Selling Ideas. I am also especially indebted to Judy Linden for her excellent editorial skill and advice, which contributed greatly to the completion of this manuscript. Finally, I thank my daughters Kira and Zenia for their encouragement and help in the organization and typing of the manuscript.

CONTENTS

INTRODUCTION   9

Part I: TAKING INVENTORY   13

Left/Right Brain Orientation. Value Orientations. Attitudes
Toward Work. Problem Solving Behaviors. Childhood-Ado-
lescence. Interests. Interpersonal Relations. Personality Dimensions. Self-perception Checklist. Negative Self-images.

Part II: BLOCKS AND BARRIERS
          TO CREATIVITY   45

Personal Blocks: Faulty Attitude Toward Problems. Lack of
Self-confidence. Fear of Criticism. Mistaken Notions About
Success. Tendency to Compare. Early Negative Condition-
ing. Lack of Self-knowledge. Lack of Positive Feelings and
Emotions. Need for the Familiar. Desire or Enforcement to
Conform. Excessive Togetherness/Fear of Solitude. Exces-
sive Future/Past Orientation. Emotional Numbness.

Problem Solving Blocks: Grabbing the First Idea. Premature
Judgments. Solution-mindedness. Overmotivation. Incessant
Effort. Concrete- or Practical-mindedness. Intolerance of
Complexity. Habit Transfer. Inability to Suspend Critical

Judgment. Poor Problem Solving Approaches. Lack of Disciplined Effort.

Environmental-Organizational Blocks: Clinging to the Established. Resistance to New Ideas. Smugnosis. Threat to Security and Status. Transgression into Private Domains. Dependency Feelings. No Time for Creative Thinking. Competition vs. Cooperation. Lack of Interest in Problems. Fantasy Making Is Worthless. Busy-ness. Isolation of the Creative Person. Fear That Ideas Will Be Stolen. Risky Road of Organizational Channels. Inability to Enlist Involvement. Other Blocks and Barriers.

**Part III: CHARACTERISTICS OF THE
           CREATIVE INDIVIDUAL   103**

Fluency. Flexibility. Sensitivity to Problems. Originality. Curiosity. Openness to Feelings and the Unconscious. Motivation. Persistence and Concentration. Ability to Think in Images. Ability to Toy with Ideas. Ability to Analyze and Synthesize. Tolerance of Ambiguity. Discernment and Selectivity. Ability to Tolerate Isolation. Creative Memory. Background of Fundamental Knowledge. Incubation. Anticipation of Productive Periods. Ability to Think in Metaphors. Aesthetic Orientation. Other Characteristics.

Part IV: POST-TEST   161

**Part V: CREATIVITY AT WORK: THE
           POLITICS OF SELLING IDEAS   187**

INTRODUCTION

WE ARE NOW CONFRONTING an accelerating rate of change in new technologies, socio-economic trends, and new attitudes and values. The "enervating eighties" promise to bring us, among other problems and challenges: (1) economic uncertainty, (2) rising costs, (3) scarcity of resources, (4) sharper competition, (5) a greater influence of international events in domestic affairs, (6) quicker paced demographic changes, (7) rising consumer discontent, (8) greater emphasis on the quality of work life, (9) the specter of more government regulation, and (10) growing employee discontent with the corporate world of work.

To cope with the uncertainty and complexity that these and other new situations, challenges and problems present, everyone needs to become more creative, imaginative and resourceful. The crucial question is, are you creative enough to meet tomorrow's challenges?

Part I of this book presents you with ten C.Q. (creativity quotient) inventories that enable you to determine if you have the personality traits, attitudes, values, motivations, problem solving skills and interests that best equip you to handle creatively new and difficult situations.

Unlike I.Q. and task-oriented tests, which have traditionally measured the conscious, analytical, cognitive, verbal, linear, logical and sequential abilities associated with the left hemisphere of our brains, the C.Q. inventories in this book are designed to go beyond these functions and measure, in addition to the above, the potentials of the less dominant and less developed capacities of the right hemisphere of our brains: the unconscious, affective, spatial, relational, concrete and aesthetic functions. The tests are based on several years' study of the characteristics and attributes possessed by men and women—across a broad spectrum of occupations and careers—that predispose them to think and act creatively.

Should you score below your expectations, remember that your C.Q. is not immutably fixed. With the help of this book you will be able to learn new attitudes, values and ways of approaching and solving problems that will considerably enhance your creative powers and talents. Especially valuable are the many exercises, scattered throughout Part III of this book, that will help you develop, extend and expand your unused creative capacities.

How vitally important continuous practice and exercise of creative techniques really are, was proved in several recent follow-up studies I made of individuals who had been trained in my creative workshop/seminars. I had been, for some time, particularly chagrined and perplexed by the relatively rapid decline of some of the participants' creative performance after they had completed the course. At first I ascribed it to the "wash-out" effect that occurred when they returned to their stuffy and unreceptive organizational climates. But then I noted that many other individuals who had received the training actually continued to increase their innovative skills *in spite* of adverse organizational situations. Further probing revealed that these individuals had continued, on their own, to practice and exercise daily the techniques they had learned. Because hands-on practice and involvement in creative games and exercises is so important, I am going to recommend my two previous books, *Creative Growth Games* and *More Creative Growth Games*, even at the risk of appearing blatantly self-promoting.

The creative urge is one of our strongest mainsprings. The veracity of this statement can be observed in individuals whose creative urge is thwarted or blocked. The creatively blocked individual is often depressed, negativistic and self-destructive. His existence is passive, purposeless and inert. He is overly dependent on other people, overly conforming to others' expectations, wishes and values. When really difficult problems develop, he tends to become confused, unproductively restless and disorganized. Although intensely preoccupied with what other people think of him, what they want from him, and how they expect him to behave, the creatively blocked person feels intense emotional isolation. Creative blockage strikes at the very root of the satisfaction in living.

The creatively free person, on the other hand, is an autonomous, self-directive individual who honors his own independent values, interests and needs. His tremendous inner resources are readily available and he can mobilize them easily when faced with serious problems or situations. He has the ability or "ego strength" to accept conflict and tension and deal with them effectively. He is frank, friendly and open in his dealings with others, yet, at the same time, he is not strongly influenced by others' expectations.

Creativity, contrary to firmly entrenched folklore, is *not* the province or preserve of only a few talented individuals in the arts, the sciences and certain other "creative professions." Many experiments conducted over the past decade have conclusively proven that creative ability is well-nigh universal, that it is built into the human species and that in almost everything we do we *can* be creative. One can be creative as a mother, cook, homemaker; one can be creative in business, social service, teaching, athletics—in fact, in almost every field and activity that exists. As the late psychologist Abraham H. Maslow described one of his acquaintances:

> . . . one woman, uneducated, poor, a full-time housewife and mother, did none of these conventionally creative things and yet was a marvellous cook, mother, wife, and homemaker. With little money, her home was somehow always beautiful. She was a perfect hostess. Her meals were banquets. Her taste in linens, silver, glass, crockery, and furniture was impeccable. She was in all these areas original, novel, ingenious, unex-

pected, inventive. I just had to call her creative. I learned from her and others like her to think that a first-rate soup is more creative than a second-rate painting.

It has also been demonstrated that the more fully creative a person's experiences and activities are, the more fulfilling they are of his life. The creative approach is a direct, positive, assertive, involved approach to life. It helps a person to become more than he is now, or could become, without exercising his inherent creative ability. The creative approach to life is at the core of healthy maturation and personality development. All healthy people want to grow, expand, develop, and express all the capacities they possess. That is why, in psychologist Erich Fromm's words, "education for creativity is nothing short of education for living." And in these words is also summed up the purpose of this book.

EUGENE RAUDSEPP
President
Princeton Creative Research, Inc.
Princeton, N.J.

*The era of the "intelligent man/woman" is
almost over and a new one is emerging—
the era of the "creative man/woman."*
PINCHAS NOY

*He who knows others is clever; he who
knows himself is enlightened.*
LAO-TSE

Life is an endless process of self-discovery.
JAMES GARDNER

PART I

Taking Inventory

LET'S BEGIN BY TAKING inventory of your creative "stock," the
assets and attributes that foster inventive thinking and allow
you to handle successfully new and difficult situations.

The ten creativity inventories that follow measure how
creative you are at the present time. The inventories are as
follows:

I.	Left/Right Brain Orientation
II.	Value Orientations
III.	Attitudes Toward Work
IV.	Problem Solving Behaviors
V.	Childhood-Adolescence
VI.	Interests
VII.	Interpersonal Relations
VIII.	Personality Dimensions

IX.   Self-perception Checklist
X.   Negative Self-images

The inventories consist of 3 checklists and 206 statements.
Scores and Subscores follow each individual inventory. Place
a check mark beside each of your responses on the checklists.
After each statement indicate with a letter whether or not
you agree with the statement:

A = Agree
B = In-between or Don't know
C = Disagree

Mark your answers as accurately and frankly as possible.
Try not to second guess how a creative person might respond
to each statement. There is no time limit.

I. LEFT/RIGHT BRAIN ORIENTATION

Recent scientific research shows that the two hemispheres of the human brain mediate and process different kinds of information and handle different kinds of tasks and problems.

Our first inventory will determine whether you are right brain oriented, left brain oriented, or if you use the "whole brain," both hemispheres, when dealing with facts, ideas and issues.

Place a check mark next to your response.

1. In auditoriums, movie theaters, lecture halls, etc., do you prefer to sit:
   - A. _____on the right side?
   - B. _____on the left side?
   - C. _____in the middle?

2. When responding to a question requiring some thought, do you:
   - A. _____tend to look to the left?
   - B. _____tend to look to the right?
   - C. _____tend to look directly at the person?

3. Are you:
   - A. _____more extraverted?
   - B. _____more introverted?

4. Are you:
   - A. _____more of a "day person"?
   - B. _____more of a "night person"?
   - C. _____both equally?

5. From the following list of characteristics and skills useful in work, identify *four* that you especially possess or are good at, and *four* that you find difficult. Designate "good" with *G*, and difficult with *D*.

   A. Managing time_____
   B. Organizing projects_____
   C. Strategic planning_____
   D. Creative problem solving_____
   E. Persuading others_____
   F. Exercising initiative_____
   G. Supervising others_____
   H. Conceptualizing_____
   I. Controlling_____
   J. Having drive/motivation_____
   K. Exercising self-discipline_____
   L. Developing programs_____
   M. Meeting deadlines_____
   N. Budgeting_____
   O. Integrating_____
   P. Motivating others_____
   Q. Consulting_____
   R. Courteousness_____
   S. Perception_____
   T. Responsiveness_____
   U. Foresightedness_____
   V. Dependability_____
   W. Insight_____
   X. Practicality_____
   Y. Energy_____
   Z. Intuitiveness_____

6. From the following list of words check *five* that best describe you:

   A. Analytical_____
   B. Logical_____
   C. Musical_____
   D. Artistic_____
   E. Mathematical_____
   F. Verbal_____
   G. Innovative_____
   H. Intuitive_____

I. Self-controlled_____
J. Detail-minded_____
K. Emotional_____
L. Able to grasp "wholes" (holistic)_____
M. Dominant_____
N. Intellectual_____
O. Able to synthesize_____
P. Spatially oriented_____
Q. Linearly oriented_____
R. A reader_____
S. A synthesizer_____
T. Able to use analogies_____

7. From the following list of phrases, check *four* that most apply to you:
   A. I have strong leadership ability._____
   B. I prefer to work independently._____
   C. I tend to be outgoing and sociable._____
   D. I have great love for the arts._____
   E. I am conscientious and responsible._____
   F. I consider myself quite sensitive._____
   G. I like to participate in team or group efforts._____
   H. I'm not very well organized._____
   I. I have good social poise._____
   J. I'm frequently critical of myself._____
   K. I respect social conventions and values._____
   L. I sometimes have doubts about my intellectual efficiency._____

Circle and add up the values you have checked.

1. A = 1; B = 10; C = 5
2. A = 10; B = 1; C = 5
3. A = 2; B = 8
4. A = 2; B = 8; C = 5
5. A. G = 2; D = 7
   B. G = 7; D = 2
   C. G = 2; D = 7
   D. G = 8; D = 2
   E. G = 2; D = 8

F. G = 7; D = 2
G. G = 2; D = 7
H. G = 7; D = 2
I. G = 2; D = 8
J. G = 7; D = 2
K. G = 2; D = 7
L. G = 7; D = 2
M. G = 1; D = 8
N. G = 2; D = 7

O. G = 7; D = 2		K = 7
P. G = 2; D = 7		L = 8
Q. G = 7; D = 2		M = 3
R. G = 1; D = 8		N = 3
S. G = 8; D = 2		O = 8
T. G = 2; D = 7		P = 8
U. G = 7; D = 3		Q = 2
V. G = 2; D = 7		R = 5
W. G = 8; D = 3		S = 8
X. G = 2; D = 8		T = 8
Y. G = 7; D = 3	7.	A = 2
Z. G = 8; D = 2		B = 8
6. A = 3		C = 2
B = 2		D = 8
C = 9		E = 2
D = 9		F = 7
E = 3		G = 3
F = 4		H = 7
G = 8		I = 3
H = 8		J = 7
I = 2		K = 3
J = 3		L = 7

YOUR SCORE:

41–84	85–128	129–172
Left Brain oriented	Double-Dominant	Right Brain oriented

The left hemisphere (in our culture the more dominant and "overdeveloped") specializes in verbal and numerical information processed sequentially in a linear fashion. It is the active, verbal, logical, rational and analytic part of our brain. The right hemisphere is associated primarily with those activities we consider to be creative. It is the intuitive, experimental, nonverbal part of our brain and it deals in images and holistic, relational grasping of complex configurations and structures. It creates metaphors, analogies and new combinations of ideas. The following gives a more detailed comparison of the Left/Right Brain functions and modes.

Comparison of Left/Right Hemisphere Functions

Left Mode	*Right Mode*
Logical, analytical, sequential, linear—drawing conclusions based on logical order of things; figuring things out in a sequential order, step-by-step, part-by-part, one element after another in an ordered way; proceeding in terms of linked thoughts, one idea directly following another, leading to a convergent conclusion; going from premises to conclusions in a series of orderly, logical steps. Utilizing precise, exact connotations—right/wrong, yes/no, etc.	Intuitive, holistic, gestalt, nonlinear—utilizing intuitive feeling of how things fit, belong or go together, making leaps of insight based on hunches, feelings, incomplete data, patterns, imagery; perceiving through pattern recognition and spatial references where things are in relation to other things and how parts connect to form wholes; holographic perception and recognition of gestalts, overall patterns, structures, configurations, complex relationships—all at once, simultaneously; multiple processing of information—arriving at conclusions without proceeding through logical, intermediary steps. Recognition of complex figures and abstract patterns.
Convergent thinking—one conclusion or alternative, one meaning.	Divergent thinking—many conclusions or alternatives, many meanings.
Rational—basing conclusions on facts and reason.	Nonrational—does not require basis of reason or facts.
Conscious processing.	Subconscious or preconscious processing.
Literal meaning.	Metaphorical/analogical meaning—perceiving likenesses between disparate things, grasping of metaphoric likenesses.
Verbal, semantic—language, speech, counting, naming, reading.	Nonverbal—use of imagery.
Abstract—selectively separat-	Concrete—relating to things or

Left Mode	Right Mode
ing a small part or subsystem and having it represent the whole.	whole-systems as they are, in the here-and-now.
Causal.	Acausal.
Explicit.	Tacit.
Controlled, consistent.	Emotive, affect-laden.
Realistic thinking—strong reality orientation.	Fantasy, reverie, daydreaming.
Dominant (usually).	Nondominant (quiet).
Intellectual, formal.	Sensuous, experiential.
Sharp focal awareness.	Diffuse awareness.
Active.	Receptive.
Linear time—keeping track of time, sequencing one thing after another.	Timelessness, nontemporal—without sense of time.
Mathematical, scientific.	Artistic, musical, symbolic.
Directed.	Free, associational, tolerant of ambiguity.
Propositional.	Imaginative.
Objective.	Subjective.
Public knowledge.	Private, idiosyncratic knowledge.
Judgmental, evaluative.	Nonjudgmental, noncritical—willing to suspend judgment.

In current discussions about the differentiation between the mental processing of the two hemispheres of the brain, the tendency is to "overvalue" the creative capabilities of the right hemisphere. It seems highly probable, however, that what we should aim at is the utilization and education of the "whole brain," the double-dominant mode. What occurs in creative thinking and problem solving is an oscillating, iterative, switching back and forth type of processing, and sometimes even a "synchronous," or simultaneous, usage of both hemispheres, rather than an exclusive or predominant emphasis on the right hemisphere.

II. VALUE ORIENTATIONS

A = Agree
B = In-between or Don't know
C = Disagree

1. I often scrutinize and think about my personal values. _____
2. It is important for me to have my own philosophy of life. _____
3. I often feel that I am cheated and victimized by life. _____
4. I sometimes wonder just who I am. _____
5. I'm attracted to the mystery of life. _____
6. I think I have a preestablished purpose in life. _____
7. We should accept religious principles on faith, and not try to scrutinize them rationally. _____
8. I have a less dogmatic and more relativistic view of life than most people. _____
9. I often wonder whether the struggle of life is inherently worthwhile. _____
10. Much of what is most important in life cannot be expressed in words. _____
11. I think that a person can be punished for sins after death. _____
12. I find philosophical discussions boring. _____
13. I often feel as if my life were in suspense, waiting for some unknown thing to happen. _____
14. I feel that my life lacks completeness and closure. _____
15. For most questions there is just one right answer. _____

16. Our country would be better off if youth were disciplined more severely. _____
17. I feel that laws should be strictly enforced. _____
18. At times I wonder whether I belong to the immediate life around me as others seem to belong. _____
19. Many problems that I encounter in life cannot be resolved in terms of right or wrong solutions. _____
20. There is no purpose already built into human life; man determines that himself. _____

Circle and add up the values for each item.

	A	B	C		A	B	C
1.	+2	0	−1	11.	−1	0	+1
2.	+2	0	−1	12.	−1	0	+1
3.	−1	0	+1	13.	+1	0	−1
4.	+1	0	−1	14.	+1	0	−1
5.	+2	0	−1	15.	−2	0	+2
6.	−2	0	+2	16.	−1	0	+1
7.	−1	0	+1	17.	−1	0	+1
8.	+2	0	−2	18.	+1	0	−1
9.	−1	0	+1	19.	+1	0	−1
10.	+1	0	−1	20.	+1	0	−1

YOUR SUBSCORE:

III. ATTITUDES TOWARD WORK

A = Agree
B = In-between or Don't know
C = Disagree

1. I place relatively greater values on rewards such as salary and status than on "job interest" and "challenge." _____
2. I always work with a great deal of certainty that I'm following the correct procedures for solving a particular problem. _____
3. I like work that has regular hours. _____
4. One of my primary concerns is to discover the kind of work that would be most natural for me to do, most inclusive of and challenging to all my capacities. _____
5. Once I undertake a project, I'm determined to finish it, even under conditions of frustration. _____
6. Thorough planning and organization of time are mandatory for solving difficult problems. _____
7. I feel I'm living up to my abilities and goals. _____
8. I prefer to work with others in a team effort rather than solo. _____
9. I prefer specific instructions to those which leave many details optional. _____
10. I like to preplan and schedule all my activities carefully. _____
11. I concentrate harder than most people on whatever interests me. _____
12. I usually work things out for myself rather than get someone to show me. _____

13. I apply myself longer and harder in the absence of external pressure than do most people. _____

14. I seldom get behind in my work. _____

15. I don't enjoy tackling a job that might involve many unknown difficulties. _____

16. Being promoted more rapidly than the typical person is important to me. _____

17. I thoroughly enjoy work in which pure curiosity leads me from one problem to another. _____

18. I can become so absorbed in my own work and interests that I do not mind a lack of friends. _____

19. I can more easily change my interests to pursue a job or a career than I can change a job to pursue my interests. _____

20. I seldom begin work on a problem that I can only dimly sense and not yet express. _____

21. I am more inclined to derive my major satisfactions from people than from my work. _____

22. I don't mind routine work if I have to do it. _____

23. I like work in which I must influence others. _____

24. I feel I have a superior capacity to succeed in my chosen field of work. _____

25. To a great extent I prefer to do my planning on my own rather than with others. _____

26. I can maintain my motivation and enthusiasm for my projects even in the face of discouragement, obstacles or opposition. _____

27. I sometimes get so involved with a new idea that I forget to do the things I ought to be doing. _____

28. In respect to my overall achievements as of today I regard myself to be very successful. _____

29. I regard myself more as a "specialist" than a "generalist." _____

30. I always resist accepting the accustomed ways of doing things. _____

31. I'm basically self-competitive rather than competitive with others. _____

32. Opportunity to contribute something original to my field of specialization is highly important to me. _____

Circle and add up the values for each item.

	A	B	C		A	B	C
1.	−1	0	+1	17.	+1	0	−1
2.	0	+1	0	18.	+1	0	−1
3.	0	+1	0	19.	−2	0	+2
4.	+2	0	−2	20.	−1	0	+1
5.	+2	0	−2	21.	−1	0	+1
6.	+1	+2	0	22.	0	+1	+2
7.	−1	0	+1	23.	+1	+2	+3
8.	−1	0	+1	24.	+1	0	−1
9.	−1	0	+1	25.	+1	0	−1
10.	−1	0	+1	26.	+1	0	−1
11.	+2	0	−2	27.	+1	0	−1
12.	+1	+2	0	28.	0	+1	0
13.	+1	0	−1	29.	−1	0	+1
14.	−1	0	+1	30.	0	+1	0
15.	−1	0	+1	31.	+1	0	−1
16.	−1	0	+1	32.	+1	0	−1

YOUR SUBSCORE:

IV. PROBLEM SOLVING BEHAVIORS

A = Agree
B = In-between or Don't know
C = Disagree

1. I prefer tackling problems for which there are precise answers. _____
2. When problem solving, I work faster when analyzing the problem, and slower when synthesizing the information I've gathered. _____
3. When a certain approach to a problem doesn't work, I can easily drop it. _____
4. I am able to stick with difficult problems over extended periods of time. _____
5. I know how my mind works. _____
6. Intuitive hunches are unreliable guides in problem solving. _____
7. I have never felt very inspired. _____
8. I don't like to ask questions that show ignorance. _____
9. I get irritated when somebody interrupts me when I'm working on something I really enjoy. _____
10. I frequently feel that the ideas that I form seem to grow out of their own roots, as if independent of my will. _____
11. I often get my best ideas when doing nothing in particular. _____
12. Ideas often run through my head preventing sleep. _____
13. I can frequently anticipate the solution to my problems. _____

14. In evaluating information, the source of it is more important to me than the content. _____

15. I feel that a logical step-by-step method is best for solving problems. _____

16. People who are willing to entertain "crackpot" ideas are impractical. _____

17. Before tackling an important problem, I saturate myself with all I can learn about it. _____

18. Aesthetic considerations are important in creative problem solving. _____

19. I am "lost to the world" when I start working on a new idea. _____

20. I know what I must do to evoke the creative mood. _____

21. It would be a waste of time for me to ask questions if I had no hope of obtaining answers. _____

22. Complex problems and situations have no appeal to me. _____

23. When confronted with a difficult problem, I try out things that would not occur to others to try. _____

24. When brainstorming, I can think up more ideas more rapidly than can the rest of the people in the group. _____

25. I have vivid imagery. _____

26. I am more interested in novelty than most people. _____

27. I can work well, irrespective of my moods or state of being. _____

28. I am able to think like a child. _____

29. Things that I've accepted as old and familiar sometimes appear to me strange and distant. _____

30. I cannot get excited about ideas that may never lead to anything. _____

31. Inspiration has nothing to do with the successful solution of problems. _____

32. Daydreaming has provided the impetus for many of my more important projects. _____

Circle and add up the values for each item.

	A	B	C		A	B	C
1.	−1	0	+1	17.	+2	0	−2
2.	−2	0	+2	18.	+2	0	−2
3.	+1	0	−1	19.	+1	0	−1
4.	+1	0	−1	20.	+1	0	−1
5.	+1	+2	0	21.	−1	0	+1
6.	−2	0	+2	22.	−1	0	+1
7.	−2	0	+2	23.	+1	0	−1
8.	−1	0	+1	24.	+1	0	−1
9.	+1	0	−1	25.	+1	0	−1
10.	+1	0	−1	26.	+1	0	−1
11.	+1	0	−1	27.	+1	+2	0
12.	+1	+2	0	28.	+1	0	−1
13.	+1	0	−1	29.	+1	0	−1
14.	−2	0	+2	30.	−1	0	+1
15.	−2	0	+2	31.	−1	0	+1
16.	−1	0	+1	32.	+2	0	−2

YOUR SUBSCORE:

28

V. CHILDHOOD-ADOLESCENCE

A = Agree
B = In-Between or Don't know
C = Disagree

1. I was very happy in my childhood. _____
2. I tend to regard my home life and my relationship with my parents, up to the age of eighteen, as nearly perfect. _____
3. At least one of my close relatives was a very creative person. _____
4. There are more conformists than mavericks in my family. _____
5. I often expressed disagreement to one or both of my parents. _____
6. Personal success was not considered important in my family. _____
7. My parents were (are) very interested in the arts. _____
8. During my childhood I frequently initiated or participated in playing practical jokes. _____
9. My father was (is) very curious about many things. _____
10. My mother was usually very irritated when she found my toys or clothing lying around. _____
11. My parents openly encouraged me to take an interest in discovering things for myself, independently. _____
12. In my youth, I was always building or making things. _____

Circle and add up the values for each item.

	A	B	C		A	B	C
1.	−1	0	+1	7.	+1	0	−1
2.	−1	0	+1	8.	+1	0	−1
3.	+1	+2	0	9.	+1	0	−1
4.	+1	0	−1	10.	+1	0	−1
5.	+2	0	−2	11.	+1	0	−1
6.	−1	0	+1	12.	+1	0	−1

YOUR SUBSCORE:

VI. INTERESTS

A = Agree
B = In-between or Don't know
C = Disagree

1. I would rather be a chemist than an artist. _____

2. I would rather read a book about geography than psychology. _____

3. If I were a college professor, I would rather teach fact courses than those involving theory. _____

4. I have a great interest in the artistic and aesthetic fields. _____

5. I am not ashamed to express "feminine" interests (if man), or "masculine" interests (if woman), if so inclined. _____

6. I sometimes "get lost" in the library for hours on end, just browsing and looking at interesting books. _____

7. I prefer drawings that are regular, neat, clean and orderly, over those that are irregular, messy, disorderly and chaotic. _____

8. Writers who use strange and unusual words merely want to show off. _____

9. I have broader interests and am more widely informed than are most people of equal intelligence and educational background. _____

10. When reading books I often write my own comments and notes in the margins. _____

11. I have many hobbies. _____

12. Wisdom is more important than knowledge. _____

13. I can learn more from self-instruction than through taking courses. _____
14. I would enjoy editing a book more than writing a book. _____
15. I like hobbies that involve collecting things. _____
16. I would rather be a banker than a sculptor. _____
17. I enjoy reading science fiction. _____
18. I admire an influential public figure more than I do a creative artist. _____
19. I have many hobbies that require logical thinking. _____
20. An efficiency expert has a greater contribution to make to society than a musician. _____

Circle and add up the values for each item.

	A	B	C		A	B	C
1.	−1	0	+1	11.	+1	0	−1
2.	−1	0	+1	12.	+1	0	−1
3.	−1	0	+1	13.	+1	0	−1
4.	+2	0	−2	14.	−1	0	+1
5.	+2	0	−2	15.	−1	0	+1
6.	+1	0	−1	16.	−1	0	+1
7.	−1	0	+1	17.	+1	0	−1
8.	−1	0	+1	18.	−1	0	+1
9.	+2	0	−2	19.	−1	0	+1
10.	+1	0	−1	20.	−1	0	+1

YOUR SUBSCORE:

VII. INTERPERSONAL RELATIONS

A = Agree
B = In-between or Don't know
C = Disagree

1. I tend to avoid situations in which I might feel inferior. _____

2. When I'm engaged in an argument, the greatest pleasure for me would be if the person who disagrees with me became a friend, even at the price of sacrificing my point of view. _____

3. It is more important for people to agree about something than to inquire into it. _____

4. I am concerned about the impression I make on people and how they react to me. _____

5. I find that I'm often turned to for advice and reassurance. _____

6. I frequently have a difficult time remembering the names of people I meet. _____

7. When I'm in a strange group of people for the first time, I often think that they are better than I am. _____

8. I expect to be accepted by most people I meet. _____

9. Sometimes I'm sure that other people can read my thoughts. _____

10. I have only a few close friends. _____

11. Things that are obvious to others are not so obvious to me. _____

12. I often brood about the thoughtless things I have said that may have hurt other people's feelings. _____

13. People who express their feelings and emotions are either unstable or immature. _____

14. People who seem unsure and uncertain about things lose my respect. _____

15. I spend a great deal of time thinking about what others think of me. _____

16. I am more confident about my intellectual ability than my social ability. _____

17. Some of my friends are unconventional. _____

18. It is wise not to expect too much of others. _____

19. I often feel that people don't want me around. _____

20. The trouble with many people is that they don't take things seriously enough. _____

21. I can get along more easily with people if they belong to about the same social and business class as myself. _____

22. I like people who are most sure of their conclusions. _____

23. I feel that there is something lacking in the average and ordinary situation. _____

24. I feel I can readily allay other people's suspicions. _____

25. In groups, I occasionally voice opinions that seem to turn some people off. _____

26. I avoid situations in which I might be blamed for my behavior or activities. _____

27. The presence of a group stimulates me to show off my knowledge. _____

28. I feel I must be successful in the eyes of others before I can be happy. _____

29. I like people who are objective and rational. _____

30. I would find it difficult to form a close friendship with a person whose manners or appearance were somewhat repulsive. _____

31. I have the capacity to bring out the good in others. _____

32. I frequently find books more interesting than people. _____

33. People should be less dependent on one another. _____

34. I feel that I am considerably different from other people. _____

35. I find that people do not take enough time to listen to my problems. _____
36. I admire people who are neat and well ordered. _____

Circle and add up the values for each item.

	A	B	C		A	B	C
1.	−1	0	+1	19.	−1	0	+1
2.	−1	0	+1	20.	−1	0	+1
3.	−1	0	+1	21.	−1	0	+1
4.	−1	0	+1	22.	−1	0	+1
5.	+1	+2	0	23.	+1	0	−1
6.	+2	0	−2	24.	+1	0	−1
7.	−2	0	+2	25.	+2	0	−2
8.	−1	0	+1	26.	−1	0	+1
9.	−1	0	+1	27.	−1	+1	0
10.	+1	0	−1	28.	−1	0	+1
11.	+1	0	−1	29.	−1	0	+1
12.	−1	0	+1	30.	−1	0	+1
13.	−1	+1	+2	31.	+1	+2	0
14.	−1	0	+1	32.	+1	0	−1
15.	−2	0	+2	33.	+1	0	−1
16.	+1	0	−1	34.	+1	+2	0
17.	+1	0	−1	35.	−1	+1	0
18.	+1	0	−1	36.	−1	0	+1

YOUR SUBSCORE:

VIII. PERSONALITY DIMENSIONS

A = Agree
B = In-between or Don't know
C = Disagree

1. I seldom act without thinking. _____
2. More than most people, I am eager to produce immediate results and seldom spend extra time taking a broad view of things before making a decision. _____
3. I tend to get upset if things do not go as scheduled. _____
4. I always consider carefully the consequences of each of my actions. _____
5. I am very active and energetic. _____
6. I know that there is sometimes a discrepancy between the way I want to behave and the way I actually behave. _____
7. People often say that I'm somewhat absent-minded. _____
8. I am less willing to entertain and express "irrational" impulses than many others. _____
9. I tend to become very emotional when I fail at something. _____
10. I am not really too different from most people. _____
11. It doesn't bother me if people do not like me. _____
12. I am freer and less rigidly controlled than most people. _____
13. There's nothing wrong with showing off a little now and then. _____
14. I keep my things well organized. _____

15. I am more contented and less dissatisfied than most people. _____
16. I sometimes get into trouble because I'm too curious or inquisitive. _____
17. I like to stick my neck out even if it is not well warranted. _____
18. I often laugh at myself for my quirks and peculiarities. _____
19. I resent things being uncertain and unpredictable. _____
20. I never get too enthusiastic over things. _____
21. When the chips are down, I display more personal strength than most people. _____
22. I have a strong desire to be alone and to pursue my own thoughts and interests. _____
23. I have a more complex personality than most people. _____
24. I am more of an idealist than a realist. _____
25. I can easily give up immediate gain or comfort to reach the goals I have set. _____
26. I feel that I'm more introverted than extraverted. _____
27. I feel that people who strive for perfection are unwise. _____
28. I sometimes use humor as a means of avoiding negative emotions. _____
29. I can sometimes be quite severe with myself, scolding and chastising myself for my foolishness and ineptitude. _____
30. I frequently tend to forget things such as names of people, streets, highways, small towns, etc. _____
31. The confusion and bustle of a big city annoys me. _____
32. I feel I have more problems than most people. _____
33. I always put my best foot forward. _____
34. I am a reflective and introspective person. _____
35. I can be aroused to deep anger and resentment. _____
36. I trust my feelings to guide me through experiences. _____
37. I am more apt than most people to run afoul of authority. _____

38. I usually come to conclusions rapidly and with finality. _____
39. I never dwell on my own limitations and imperfections. _____
40. Self-sufficiency is a prime requirement for a contented life. _____
41. I would rate myself high in self-confidence. _____
42. I have a great deal of initiative and ability to be self-starting. _____
43. I have great tenacity of purpose. _____
44. The room in which I work is quite cluttered and messy. _____
45. I tend to rely more on my first impressions and feelings when making judgments than on a careful analysis of the situation. _____
46. Friends consider me unconventional in many ways. _____
47. I feel that a good sense of humor is very important in life. _____
48. I have frequently sought out complex and frustrating situations. _____
49. I have restrained my curiosity. _____
50. The spontaneity and innocence of children appeals to me. _____
51. People who emphasize self-realization or self-actualization are self-centered. _____
52. I am a very "reality-oriented" person. _____
53. I never brood about problems or things. _____
54. I feel that I have, psychologically, both sicker and healthier aspects to my personality than do people in general. _____

Circle and add up the values for each item.

	A	B	C			A	B	C
1.	−1	0	+1		6.	+1	0	−1
2.	−1	0	+1		7.	+1	0	−1
3.	0	+2	+1		8.	−1	0	+1
4.	−1	0	+1		9.	−1	0	+1
5.	+1	0	−1		10.	0	+2	+1

	A	B	C			A	B	C
11.	+1	+2	0		33.	0	+1	0
12.	+1	0	+1		34.	+1	0	−1
13.	+1	0	−1		35.	+1	0	−1
14.	−1	0	+1		36.	+1	0	−1
15.	−1	0	+1		37.	+1	0	−1
16.	+2	0	−2		38.	−1	0	+1
17.	+1	0	−1		39.	−1	0	+1
18.	+1	0	−1		40.	+1	+2	0
19.	−1	0	+1		41.	+2	+1	0
20.	−2	0	+2		42.	+1	0	−1
21.	+1	0	−1		43.	+2	0	−2
22.	+2	0	−2		44.	+1	0	−1
23.	+1	0	−1		45.	+1	+2	0
24.	+1	0	−1		46.	+1	0	−1
25.	+1	0	−1		47.	+2	0	−2
26.	+1	0	−1		48.	+1	0	−1
27.	−1	+1	0		49.	−1	0	+1
28.	+1	0	−1		50.	+1	0	−1
29.	+1	0	−1		51.	−1	0	+1
30.	+1	0	−1		52.	0	+2	+1
31.	−1	0	+1		53.	0	+2	+1
32.	−1	0	+1		54.	+2	0	−2

YOUR SUBSCORE:

IX. SELF-PERCEPTION CHECKLIST

Below is a list of adjectives and terms that describe people. Indicate with a check mark *twelve* words that best describe you.

_____ energetic
_____ persuasive
_____ observant
_____ fashionable
_____ self-confident
_____ persevering
_____ forward-looking
_____ cautious
_____ habit-bound
_____ resourceful
_____ egotistical
_____ independent
_____ good-natured
_____ predictable
_____ formal
_____ informal
_____ dedicated
_____ original
_____ quick
_____ efficient
_____ helpful
_____ perceptive
_____ courageous
_____ stern
_____ thorough

_____ factual
_____ open-minded
_____ tactful
_____ inhibited
_____ enthusiastic
_____ innovative
_____ poised
_____ acquisitive
_____ practical
_____ alert
_____ curious
_____ organized
_____ unemotional
_____ clear-thinking
_____ understanding
_____ dynamic
_____ self-demanding
_____ polished
_____ realistic
_____ modest
_____ involved
_____ absentminded
_____ flexible
_____ sociable
_____ well-liked

The following have values of +2:

energetic
observant
persevering
resourceful
independent
dedicated
original
perceptive
enthusiastic
innovative
curious
involved
flexible

The following have values of +1:

self-confident
forward-looking
informal
courageous
thorough
open-minded
alert
dynamic
self-demanding
absentminded

The rest have values of 0.

Add up the values for each item checked.

YOUR SUBSCORE:

X. NEGATIVE SELF-IMAGES

Following is a list of relatively *negative* terms that are used to describe people. Indicate with a check mark the one term of each pair that is closest to describing you, or is less offensive to your self-image. Remember, even if neither term really describes you, select the one of each pair that is nearest to what conceivably could be your negative trait. Be sure to check one of *each* pair of choices.

1. _____ Impulsive
   _____ Worrying
2. _____ Messy
   _____ Dogmatic
3. _____ Sarcastic
   _____ Rigid
4. _____ Masochistic
   _____ Uncooperative
5. _____ Obstinate
   _____ Complacent
6. _____ Habit-bound
   _____ Arrogant
7. _____ Naive
   _____ Impractical
8. _____ Asocial
   _____ Domineering
9. _____ Hypocritical
   _____ Meek
10. _____ Lone wolf
    _____ Modest

11. _____ Daydreamer
    _____ Humble
12. _____ Opportunistic
    _____ Unenthusiastic
13. _____ Passive
    _____ Emotional
14. _____ Frivolous
    _____ Obsequious
15. _____ Authoritarian
    _____ Moody
16. _____ Cautious
    _____ Credulous
17. _____ Overly-sensitive
    _____ Inhibited
18. _____ Machiavellian
    _____ Pedantic
19. _____ Conformist
    _____ Sadistic
20. _____ Guilt-ridden
    _____ Zany

Score one point for each of the following traits you checked:

1.	Impulsive_____	11.	Daydreamer_____
2.	Messy_____	12.	Opportunistic_____
3.	Sarcastic_____	13.	Emotional_____
4.	Uncooperative_____	14.	Frivolous_____
5.	Obstinate_____	15.	Moody_____
6.	Arrogant_____	16.	Credulous_____
7.	Impractical_____	17.	Overly-sensitive_____
8.	Asocial_____	18.	Machiavellian_____
9.	Hypocritical_____	19.	Sadistic_____
10.	Lone wolf_____	20.	Zany_____

YOUR SUBSCORE:

To compute your total score, add up your nine subscores.

Your Total Score:

243–303	Exceptionally creative
153–242	Very creative
68–152	Above average
36–67	Average
12–35	Below average
−210−−11	Noncreative

*Most everybody keeps the body fit nowa-
days.
But not many try to keep the brain fit too.*
FRED JACOB

*The buried talent is the sunken rock on
which most lives strike and founder.*
FREDERICK W. FABER

*Every healthy and creative individual
resists engulfment by custom and rigid
habits.*
HERBERT BONNER

PART II

Blocks and Barriers to Creativity

PERHAPS YOU DIDN'T do as well as you anticipated on the inventories. There's really no need to be alarmed since this is not so much due to the absence of creative potential as it is to the various blocks and barriers that tend to inhibit, stifle, distort, narrow and discourage effective creative activity. Luckily, once the barriers have been recognized and identified, and a conscious effort is made to remove them, the immediate upsurge of creative output can be considerable.

In a sense, the problem can be likened to a gutter under the eaves of a roof, clogged with dead leaves, twigs, bugs and sediment. In order for the rainwater to flow through, the gutter must first be cleared. In a similar way, free flowing creativity and receptivity to new ideas also require the elimination of personal and environmental sediments.

While gaining insight into most blocks is sufficient for us to make better and more productive use of our latent creative talents, there are some emotional blocks that are difficult to recognize in ourselves, difficult to admit and overcome, even in our best interests. Facing them in a conscious, open way, however, and regarding them as challenges and problems to solve, enables us to move toward a more creative life-style.

PERSONAL BLOCKS

Faulty Attitude Toward Problems

Life is full of problems and difficulties. To consider the ideal condition of life a Nirvana-like state is illusory. A human being is not a vegetable or an inanimate object. Because he or she can think, feel, respond, remember, plan, move forward; because he or she is a social being intimately involved with others in the enterprise of living, a life without problems, difficulties and challenges, without aspirations and striving against odds, would offer no sustenance to inherent humanness and creative potentialities. For a healthy, fully functioning human being, problems, snags, difficulties, barriers, are integral and essential parts of living which act as *challenges* to test and develop creative capacities. The healthy creative individual welcomes challenges; he actually feeds upon problems and actively seeks them out for the gratifying experience of gaining mastery over them.

Most noncreative people have one cardinal trait in common: they are passive. They *react* to situations and events, rather than creatively *acting* to bring about new circumstances and situations. They expect happiness to descend upon them through the fiat of some lucky break. Since this kind of happiness rarely occurs, they tend to blame outside circumstances or other people for their unhappiness. They cannot see or admit that the real cause of their discontent lies basically in themselves. Even if external circumstances are difficult, it is their *chronic unwillingness to do something effective about their situation* that allows the feeling of un-happiness to persist. Only when a person has decided to break out of the self-negating rut, when he begins to tackle his problem actively and creatively has he begun to lay a firm foundation to his psychological health and happiness.

Always protecting oneself from unpleasantnesses, fail-ures, disappointments and hurts will not enable one to be-come strong and healthy. Just as in preventive medicine poi-son is injected into the living body to build up immunity, so in life the creative acceptance of the inevitable "poisons" of life will make a person less vulnerable to disappointments and failures and more resistant to misfortunes.

Most creative people possess a certain spirit of adventur-ousness, a genuine willingness to take chances. By adopting this attitude, they almost automatically open and free their imaginations and conquer fear. The essence of creative growth and zestful living lies in the willingness to occasional-ly leap into the unknown, a willingness to give up temporarily the rigid routine of one's living and the solidified habit pat-terns that make the future seem secure and predictable. While life is full of risks, it is also full of promises. To partake of the latter, however, a person has to be willing to stick his neck out and take some risks. Balance or wholeness in life is not achieved by shrinking from experience in order to pre-serve the mold into which one's life is cast; it is achieved by increasing the variety and range of inner and outer life by immersing oneself unhesitatingly in fresh, new experiences. As has been well put: "The only self worth having is one that is interested in many things beyond itself."

Lack of Self-confidence

It is seldom recognized how much self-confidence and ego strength a person requires to do justice to his or her inherent creative potential. Indeed, one of the most serious blocks that inhibits, and sometimes even nips the budding career of a novice, is a lack of inner confidence. This expresses itself as doubt about one's abilities, or fear of being compared with others; fear of appearing foolish or unusual; fear of failing to sustain a commitment when faced with adverse circumstances and fear of making a mistake.

Rare indeed is the established creative person (and even rarer the beginner) who can consistently maintain a complete detachment from negative opinions. Yet to call one's own shots and to stick to one's convictions in the face of possible discouragement or censure is very necessary in creative work.

Self-confidence can best be developed through experience and exercise. It has been said that nothing breeds success like success, and this is probably true, but the corollary that failure breeds failure need not be true. If through continued and persistent application failures are corrected, high orders of self-confidence and optimism can be achieved. Good creative judgment comes only with experience. And experience inevitably entails some bad creative judgment. We should realize that creative progress is made through failures and bad judgment as well as through successes and good judgment.

Self-confidence cannot be built up entirely alone. A young person especially needs a healthy dose of encouragement and ego-boosting recognition to develop the belief that he will succeed eventually, no matter how many times he may fail initially. In time, luckily, most creative people attain a solid confidence in their ideas, work and capabilities. Once they have attained this level of confidence, there no longer exists a serious threat to the self; situations are perceived and weighed realistically, and there is a ready willingness to risk failure and give free rein to the powers of imagination.

One of the best ways to restore or reaffirm healthy self-confidence is to take stock of our past achievements. With this in mind, briefly write down four of your most significant achievements to date, either on the job or in your personal life. Describe what was achieved, why you did it, when you did it, where you did it, who was involved, what difficulties, if any, you overcame, etc.

After you have them written down, decide which of the

four is your most important achievement. Would you want to do it again? Could you surpass it today? Briefly write down what you want to be your next achievement.

Fear of Criticism

Because creativity is, in a sense, destructive of the established and accepted, and because there is a natural human tendency to maintain the status quo, the more unique and original an idea is, the more vulnerable it becomes to destructive criticism or censorship.

People are, by and large, extremely sensitive to any overt or implied criticism of their ideas. One seldom encounters a person who has a completely unemotional and objective attitude toward his ideas—who could benefit from criticism that is justified and helpful and ignore the rest. However tough a person may outwardly be, overcritical attitudes, or expressions of cynicism, ridicule or just plain indifference do have an inhibiting effect. They repress original ideas, and, in extreme cases, produce a "drought"—a period in which no new ideas emerge even in the privacy of the individual's own mind.

It is essential that the aspiring creative person learn to evaluate criticism both for content and intent, keeping in mind that people are subject to a variety of pressures which makes them behave irrationally and destructively. With this degree of objectivity achieved and with the realization that one's idea often is *not* the target of criticism, it will be possible to utilize constructive offerings and discard the petty or misplaced.

Mistaken Notions About Success

Many people in our society show an inordinate capacity for setting up false expectations, self-defeating goals and illusory objectives—all based on faulty notions about what constitutes success. One of these faulty expectations is that once you gain wealth, power and fame, you've got it made. Ask almost anyone you know to describe what success means to him or her, and the chances are that the majority of responses would fall into the category of material acquisitions. When William James observed around the turn of the century that "the exclusive worship of the bitch-goddess Success is our national disease," he was referring to the still prevalent idolatry of material success and fame.

Yet, the fact is that a great many of the rich who have it made in material terms, rarely, if ever, attribute their wellbeing to wealth. And there are, of course, many wealthy people who, in spite of all the accoutrements of outward riches and success, look as miserable as if they hadn't a thing in the world. They always scramble after more and are chronically dissatisfied with what they have. Their lives point to one of the most pernicious aspects of material possessions: the buildup of an unquenchable thirst for more.

There are many other unfortunate aspects to the single-minded pursuit of material success. Scrambling after material wealth teaches many people to be shrewd, ruthless, crafty and expedient. They are frequently insensitive toward others and possess an opportunistic, self-seeking streak that pervades almost everything they do. Then there are those who, in order to achieve material success, are willing to distort and compromise their values and convictions to curry favor with those in positions of wealth and power. By denying their real selves they become empty husks, the hollow repositories of other people's expectations and demands.

Of late, a healthy development is taking place. An increasing number of people have begun to seriously question the dogma and worship of our popular forms of success, and they openly recognize that their values, interests and goals diverge radically from the materialistic mainstream.

In the final analysis, success is a totally personal ideal, and each of us gives different definitions to the term. Psychologist Lila Swell defines success this way: "A success is any event or experience that you remember as self-fulfilling. It can be a physical, social, intellectual or aesthetic experience—any event that made you feel successful, good, useful, and/or important." Her definition shows that there are many other dimensions to success than just possessions, fame, status and popularity.

The creative individual has a strong and vibrant success orientation. It is directed toward extending the range and quality of those experiences that bring him a sense of accomplishment and a feeling of self-fulfillment. His life requires an endless sequence of new challenges, directions and goals. Utilizing fully his creative and inventive capacities, he wants his life to become a series of continuous self-creations in which he takes an active part.

Tendency to Compare

The creative individual is true to himself, true to his inner nature. He seldom has a need to compare his abilities or his creative achievements to those of others. He is realistically aware of his capacities as well as his limitations and is in competition *only* with himself, with his previous creative accomplishments. There are so many gradations of achievement and success in our complex world that simple and valid comparisons are almost impossible to make.

There is hardly a surer way to diminish the joy of creative attainment than to compare our achievements with those of someone else. An individual who makes a habit of comparing his accomplishments to those of others is inhibited in his creative undertakings and can never fully savor his creative feats, no matter how great they are. This is because the act of comparison hampers the mind and makes every success relative. Measuring your creative performance against the yardstick of someone else's performance can even mean that your brainchild is a relative failure.

Early Negative Conditioning

Creativity can easily become blocked quite early in life through the unthinking remarks and behavior of adults. The following "case histories," suggested by psychiatrist O. Spurgeon English, illustrate the negative influence unenlightened parenting can have.

Consider the example of a ten-year-old child who was trying to write stories. When she tried to get her mother to listen the latter said impatiently, "Who would want to read the trash that a ten-year-old would write?" As a result of a few rebuffs such as this, the child naturally retired from attempts at writing and never was able to do anything creative later in life even though she had latent interest.

Another case involves a youngster who begged his father for a house for his dog. The father bought the materials and the boy looked forward with great anticipation to the day when he and his father would build the doghouse together. But the father did not want his nine-year-old son "in the way," so he assembled the doghouse while his son was at the movies with a friend. The boy returned home only to find the job completed. His disappointment was lost on the father who was pleased with himself at having finished the construction. Actually, the father wished to be relieved of the trouble of patiently standing by and of sharing in his son's amateurish but valuable early efforts in creation. Pity the children who have never made anything with their hands and received their parents' admiration!

Another clear-cut block to creativity is seen in the history of a young man in his late teens who was beset by doubt, indecision and feelings of inferiority because his parents had repeatedly asked him, whatever his undertaking, "Do you think you can do it?" Their distrust of his ability to pursue a good thought, a useful idea, a constructive endeavor had infiltrated his mind so thoroughly that he was paralyzed and totally unequal to healthy action, whether mental or physical.

Still another example is that of a woman whose ideas and opinions were belittled throughout her childhood. During the dinner hour, for example, a subject would be under discussion and she would venture an opinion, wishing to participate. To this her father would say, "What does a child like you know about it?" Or "Of what value, do you think, is an adolescent's opinion to people our age who know about these things?" As might be expected, this woman is silent and inhibited in formation and expression of opinions today at the age of forty-five.

From such experiences come the blocks, the fears, guilts, inhibitions, and projections of old hurts that are truly inimical to creativity. Not only are these wounded people fearful of criticism such as they received as children, but any attempt at creative work immediately evokes massive guilt feelings that they may be competing with, or even attempting to overthrow, a parental figure from his or her position of authority.

Lack of Self-knowledge

An increasing number of people these days are asking themselves the all-important questions: "Who am I really?" "Where am I going?" "What should I be doing to lead a creative and zestful life?" "Am I living in a way that is truly satisfying?" As these questions indicate, the primary need for the contemporary man or woman seems to be the need to discover the basic requirements of his or her innermost nature. People, these days, urgently desire to embark on the road to self-discovery, toward the full exercise and expression of inherent creative individuality. In short, they want to regain the initiative for life.

The road to self-knowledge and the expression of true individuality is not easy. As long ago as the sixth century B.C. Heraclitus observed: "Man is estranged from that with which he is most familiar, and he must continuously seek to rediscover it." Of course, in our times the rediscovery of our real selves is doubly hard because most of us have learned to be more concerned with what we *should* do and be, with what is *expected* from us, than with our true creative inclinations and needs. Governed, as most of us are, by "other-directions," by conventions and tradition, we have lost touch with our inner selves.

That self-knowledge is the basis of psychological health and creative individuality has been attested by psychologist Carl R. Rogers. From thousands of persons he has treated he concludes that behind almost every patient's problem is one central, universal theme: "What is my real self?" "How can I get in touch with this real self, underlying all my surface behavior?" "How can I become myself?"

In his therapeutic technique, progress is recorded when the person begins to act more like his true self, dropping the false masks and roles he has hitherto used. Only when the person begins to realize how much of his actions have been based on his mistaken notions of what he should be or do, is he on the road to recovery. As Rogers says, "Often the person discovers that he exists *only* in response to the demands of others, that he seems to have no self of his own, that he is only trying to think, and feel, and behave in the way that others believe he ought to think and feel and behave. Once he has recognized this, half the battle is already won."

According to recent research, individuals who succeed in becoming more aware of their true inner needs are more capable of assuming creative self-responsibility. Psychologist Stella Resnick puts it this way:

Self-responsibility means recognizing that you choose what you do and who you are. When individuals take responsibility for their lives, they enlarge their alternatives and learn to make choices that enhance and nourish them rather than deplete them. . . . As people pay attention to themselves they begin to recognize how their habitual ways of thinking color their experience, limit their alternatives, and restrict their positive, nourishing, creative ways of being.

Every human being has a true inner self from which his

creative strength flows. When this inner self is allowed to "pilot the ship," the human venture can be a unique and creative voyage. But this inner self needs to be cultivated, tended to and brought to full awareness. As psychologist Magda Proskauer puts it, "Much as a gardener tends to the soil in order that his plants may grow in their own way and season, so attending to the depths of our own nature tills the soil in which, firmly rooted, we can develop into creative individuals."

Self-knowledge also implies the knowledge of what kind of impression you make on others. As soon as two people come into contact, they form an impression of one another, whether at parties, business lunches, job interviews, etc. This impression, whether positive or negative, is formed in the first few minutes, and it is frequently hard to change. One seldom gets a second chance to make a first impression.

Make copies of the following form and hand them out to friends or acquaintances who want to participate in this very revealing and fun exercise.

Each participant checks the four words on the chart opposite that best describes his or her own personality as seen by others most of the time. They then check the four characteristics they think most typical of each person present. After the ratings have been completed, each participant in turn explains why he rated himself/herself and the others as he did, and what caused him to make his choices.

Lack of Positive Feelings and Emotions

In a recent study I conducted with over 1400 people in almost all walks of life, the following two questions were posed: "What are some of the most pleasant things that have happened to you during your lifetime—things that made you feel exceptionally good about yourself and your life?" and "What are some of the most unpleasant and frustrating things that have ever happened to you during your lifetime—things that made you feel exceptionally bad about yourself and your life?" It came as somewhat of a shock that in

Place the initials of the other members
of your group in these columns.

	Self									
energetic										
gracious										
agreeable										
understanding										
confident										
observant										
soft-spoken										
reserved										
sincere										
warm										
cheerful										
tactful										
intelligent										
witty										
decisive										
dominant										
calm										
serious										
mature										
enthusiastic										
cooperative										
bold										
patient										
thoughtful										
frank										
easygoing										
modest										
responsible										
efficient										

almost every case the "pleasant things" were dispensed with in a few sentences while the "unpleasant things" elicited long and elaborate essays. This, in a sense, confirmed my impression that most people are more aware of and articulate more readily what bothers, irritates and frustrates them than what they find pleasurable.

To probe further into the "why" of this state of affairs, I next undertook a study of the known human feelings and emotions, boiled them down into eight basic, primary affect assemblies. This led to the discovery, confirmed by other researchers in the field, that the negative affect responses to living—both in their quantity and intensity-duration dimensions—predominate over the positive affect responses. They are as follows:

Positive Affects

1. Enjoyment or joy. Get pleasure from; to relish, rejoice, have a good time. A very glad pleasurable feeling. Gratification. Delight. Happiness.

2. Interest or excitement. A feeling of intentness, curiosity, excited attention. A thrilling experience. Arousal of feelings of passion and enthusiasm. Creative excitement.

3. Surprise. Feeling of wonder or astonishment. Unexpected pleasure. Amazement.

Negative Affects

4. Anger or rage. Feeling of displeasure resulting from injury, mistreatment, opposition. Revengeful displeasure. Resentment.

5. Distress or anguish. Sorrow, misery, suffering, pain, trouble, constraint, strain, worry, grief, agony. Mental anguish. Depression.

6. Fear or terror. Anxiety, dread, fright, agitation, apprehension. Feelings of uneasiness, concern. To expect with misgiving, uneasiness. Panic.

7. Shame or humiliation. Painful feelings of having lost respect of others. Hurting of pride or dignity by being caused to be or seem foolish, stupid or contemptible.

8. Contempt or disgust. Dislike, scorn, deep aversion, repugnance. Considering somebody (or oneself) low, worthless or beneath notice. Distasteful experience.

While there is little doubt that most human beings have a strong urge to live, learn and grow; communicate and be with others; seek novelty and creative mastery over life's problems; prefer excitement and joy over boredom, helplessness and the distress of loneliness—in short, to maximize the positive affects and minimize the negative affects—it nevertheless remains a difficult and never ending task because of the psychobiologically determined broader spectrum of negative affects.

Creativity requires inner quietude and the accentuation of positive feelings and emotions. One of the fundamental conditions for creativity is receptive concentration. And one cannot achieve this state when bothered by mental pollutants. We cannot readily entertain new ideas, thoughts and images when the voices of uneasiness and fear disturb us. Contradictory as it may seem, many apparently urgent personal problems and obsessive negative feelings are best resolved by putting them aside or temporarily forgetting them. This is the principle of *creative deferment*. We all tend to become obsessed by persistent personal problems. The result is that we are less able to see them clearly and act upon them realistically. Frequently, the best strategy is, instead, to substitute some constructive, creative activity in place of brooding over these problems. With the exercise of the free areas of the personality, apparently insurmountable problems get crowded out, or shrink to their proper size.

It is a good idea to keep so busy with constructive and creative activities (often in the face of what loom as overwhelming problems) that there is no time to examine and reexamine the same old issues. Then, with the gain of confidence and self-respect that constructive and productive behavior produces, the original problems (if they are still there) can be solved calmly and systematically. The previously overwhelming and blinding issues will transform themselves into new challenges—which you can then approach with a much more realistic attitude.

Need for the Familiar

With the passage of time most people tend to become more conservative and habit-prone. We build up comfortable and predictable systems or channels in which our need for stability and security can easily flow and solidify. Some of us even tend to become so "attached" or "devoted" to certain patterns and actions that we are loath to give them up, regardless of their unsuitability in specific situations. If at times something new wells forth, the conflict it creates between the old and secure and the need for new, untried modes of operation often ends with the victory of our conservative impulses, and we continue the familiar order of things. The danger inherent in this is the possibility that new and worthwhile ideas may be rejected by their originator without trial because they go against established thought or action patterns. Full awareness of this all-too-human tendency is the most effective way to combat it.

Desire or Enforcement to Conform

Conformity has become an endemic disease of our time. The "institutionalizing" of the individual (through desire or pressure to comply with groups to which he or she happens to belong) begins early, continues throughout life and results in the following:

- Dependence on the opinions of others when judging something.
- Feelings of self-respect and self-worth dependent on what others think of you.
- Stereotypical ways of acting and thinking.
- The feeling that in order to "fit in" and belong to a group one must slavishly imitate them and conform to their "rules."
- Never questioning or wondering about given directives, policies, objectives, values and ideas.
- A preference for passive observation instead of active participation.

All people are "conformists" in the sense that they share certain thought and behavior patterns. And, being creative is not being perpetually rebellious or difficult to deal with, or in constant opposition to all and any accepted ideas and methods. The type of conformity that does get in the way of creativity involves the desire to relinquish all responsibility for judgments and actions.

From personality inventories similar to the one in Part I of this book researchers have established that the extreme conformist has strong feelings of inferiority or inadequacy. He is preoccupied with what his peers and superiors think of him. Having an authoritarian outlook on life, he can be characterized as narrowly conventional. His dogmatic attitudes make him hostile and prejudiced toward "foreign" groups.

The extreme conformist is usually reluctant to accept responsibility. He has a tendency to be rigid in his thought and perception and cannot tolerate ambiguity. He is unable to make decisions involving complex issues without vacillation and delay.

Although these general characteristics are indicative of all extreme conformists, they can be manifested in different ways. Three basic types of conformists have been identified.

Other-directed conformer. This person's beliefs and judgments are based on the opinions of the group to which he (or she) belongs or identifies with. Rather than relying on his own evaluation of a situation or problem, he relies greatly on how the group perceives the situation. Reluctant to express opinions and ideas that diverge from the group, and assailed by doubts about his own ability, he is unlikely to make creative contributions.

Selective conformer. This person has his own individualistic outlook, but usually goes along with the group merely to avoid trouble. However, he *is* able to articulate his ideas and opinions in groups where they are encouraged and valued. He can turn conformity on and off at will.

As long as the selective conformer can make the fine distinctions between when it is appropriate to conform and when it is not, he can remain constructively productive. But there is a great danger that time will blunt the fine edge of this discrimination, resulting in his yielding more and more to group pressures.

Negativistic conformer. This person rejects every group or majority standard and opinion. He (or she) "conforms to nonconformity" in the name of sheer rebellion, even when the group happens to be right. Because he indulges in difference for difference's sake, his efforts are cut off from the consensual validation required of creative effort and are directed at superficial outward appearances.

While such a person may appear at first to be independent in his thinking, he is really just as dependent on the group as the other types of conformists. Since the negativistic conformer gains his identity from pulling the other way, he must rely on the group to "tell" him which way to go.

As might be expected, the personality of the constructive nonconformist is quite a bit different from that of the conformist. The constructive nonconformist is highly intelligent and original in his thought patterns. He (or she) usually possesses considerable physical and intellectual drive and is efficient in problem solving. He is flexible enough to tolerate ambiguity, which allows him to hold off coming to conclusions until most of a problem's pieces can be fitted together.

The nonconformist is self-reliant, able to think for himself, and can reach conclusions that go against the majority view. Occasionally, he can be exceedingly bold in his ideas. But he can also arrive at conventional answers for common solutions if that is where his thinking leads him. He is neither unduly susceptible to the pressures of the group nor unduly driven to alienate himself from the group.

The nonconformist is generally more spontaneous in his actions than the conformist. He displays an acute ability to empathize with other people. He is usually natural and free from pretense and arrogance. When under stress, he can mobilize his resources effectively. If he had to choose between security and a chance for growth that would mean taking some chances, he would pick the latter course.

To illustrate the point of view of the nonconformist, here are some statements that nonconformists usually agree with when taking personality tests:

- Sometimes I rather enjoy going against the rules and doing things I'm not supposed to.
- I like to fool around with new ideas, even if they turn out later to be a total waste of time.
- At times I have been so entertained by the cleverness of a crook that I have hoped he would get by with it.
- It is unusual for me to express strong disapproval or approval of the actions of others.
- Compared to my own self-respect, the respect of others means very little.

For comparison, the following statements are usually endorsed by conformists:

- I am in favor of very strict enforcement of all laws, no matter what the consequences.

- I don't like to work on a problem unless there is a possibility of coming out with a clear-cut answer.
- Once I have made up my mind I seldom change it.
- Perfect balance is the essence of all good things.
- I am often bothered by useless thoughts that keep running through my head.

Attitudes toward work. The conformist and the nonconformist respond to their working environment in a strikingly different fashion. The following description of the differences is based upon the extensive studies of Frederick I. Herzberg, professor of management at the University of Utah.

The conformist is motivated primarily by the work environment and working conditions. The nature of the work itself is of secondary importance.

The conformist tends to be chronically dissatisfied with various aspects of his work situation. His salary is low or advances are not forthcoming when they should; his superiors are incompetent; working conditions are below par; he is not accorded the status in the organizational hierarchy he thinks he deserves; he feels insecure in his job; organizational policy and administration leave much to be desired; fellow employees do not show him the respect he feels is due him.

The conformist realizes little satisfaction from accomplishment. For him (or her), a pat on the back has to be a daily occurrence. He (or she) is cynical about the virtues of work, works only where there is concrete external reward to be obtained and tends to parrot top-management's philosophy.

On the other hand, the nonconformist is motivated mainly by the nature of the work and the challenge of the projects he is assigned to. Working conditions are noticed only when they interfere with effective performance.

The nonconformist has a high tolerance for the negative aspects of his (or her) work situation. While he sometimes may consider his salary to be less than it should be, he rarely broods about it. He is capable of recognizing the positive qualities of his superiors as well as their shortcomings. He is unimpressed by status symbols, feels secure as long as he produces, and respects his associates.

The nonconformist gains great satisfaction from accomplishment. Aside from normal recognition, he (or she) has little need for praise. He has a great capacity to enjoy his work, provided it suits his interests and abilities. His main challenge is solving difficult problems.

The nonconformist's attitudes and beliefs are sincere and considered. He appreciates and is sympathetic with top-management problems, but does not overidentify with top management.

Forces that foster conformity. Several forces are active in society and the work environment that contribute to conformity. Two of them—an increase in mutual dependency and a faulty interpretation of the democratic method—are especially troublesome for the constructive nonconformist.

Mutual dependency is on the rise because of ever-increasing specialization in organizations. Confinement of the person to a very narrow sector of the total operation forces him to spend most of his energy anticipating what others *are* doing, or *will be* doing, and adjusting to changes he had no part in bringing about. These frustrating interdependencies leave little time and energy to attend to personal development.

But perhaps the most powerful force for conformity is the illusion that if a majority of people share certain ideas and accept certain conclusions, those ideas and conclusions must be correct. This glorification of the majority has the effect of endorsing the most popular view which, in turn, pressures those with minority views to conform or risk rejection.

Most organizations use "majority rule" in making decisions and evaluating new ideas and products. The danger is that an overemphasis on teamwork and consensus will inhibit the pursuit of offbeat solutions. The person who is brave enough to develop and suggest a truly different approach is often ignored or ridiculed into silence—which almost certainly ensures he won't risk being different in the future.

Another thing detrimental to the conforming individual is that his perceptions and judgments become faulty. Even when he has a number of creative choices from which to choose, he is unable to summon guidance from his true needs because he basically distrusts them. At times, to be sure, he feels a vague conflict between his real needs and his conformity-conditioned responses, but he is apt to resolve this conflict in favor of the preference rules, codes, conventions, expectations, enforcements or ideals of the group or value-system with which he identifies. He is apt to bypass his true self to assume the role that is expected of him.

Excessive Togetherness/Fear of Solitude

Our collective herd existence must be all powerful. How else can we account for the fact that many of us have almost lost our sense of privacy. Indeed, we are almost afraid to act without companionship. We instinctively reach for the television, the radio or a book when we're alone; seldom do we sit with nothing but our thoughts. In our business establishments, most employees sit in one large room, or if there are partitions, they are either made of glass to promote visual togetherness, or are short in height when opaque so the usually high noise level reassures workers that they are not really alone.

How reluctantly most of us regard leisure or relaxation in a positive fashion has been experimentally demonstrated by the widely used Thematic Apperception Test. This test consists of a series of pictures about which the subjects are asked to tell stories. These stories purport to reveal a great deal about deeper-lying attitudes and preconceptions.

One picture in this test shows a group of young men leisurely lying in the grass. Most people interpret this picture to mean that these men have been working very hard on a farm or on a highway construction project, that they decided to take a "short breather," and that they will resume working *in a few minutes*. Such stories show that most people are reluc-

66

tant to regard leisure as a very vital and positive aspect of their lives.

For zestful creative living, privacy and solitude need to be reinstated and cultivated with care. We need to retreat periodically from togetherness, from the tensions, hurry and stress of collective living and doing, and embark on a return journey into ourselves. In addition to enabling us to regain a valid perspective on our lives, it will provide us with the solitary leisure so necessary for meaningful creative thinking.

Excessive Future/Past Orientation

There are two views of life—or more precisely, "ways of feeling" about life—that really prevent our living fully and creatively. They are often so deeply ingrained and habitual that we may not even be aware of them.

The first, more common in our culture, is living in the future. The other, more characteristic of some other cultures, is living in the past. Both have similar results—loss of contact with present reality.

The individual who lives in the future generally feels helpless at the speed with which time passes; he is constantly appalled at the brevity of life. His behavior aims at something to be attained, not now, not today, but at some undetermined time in the future.

On the other hand, the person who is focused on the past complains about the slowness of time—about life's boredom and endless length. He sees little point in present action, for he has turned away from life; he looks backward. It is apparent that, in either case, the existential "here and now" is lost. And yet, the present moment is the only time that we can truly call our own.

Enjoying the immediate experience is necessary to a creative and zestful life. To make our living more enjoyable, the first essential step is to restore the sense of "here and now."

We must learn how to make every hour count. Only then will each day become meaningful and enriching.

Everyone has had the occasional experience of "losing himself" in some activity. When you are fully concentrated on the present, creatively engrossed in what you are doing, the feeling of onrushing time vanishes. That experience is the result of the total absorption of your personality in a creative "here and now" activity. This was not because of its promise in terms of future rewards or gains, but because it was, in itself, engrossing or interesting.

By contrast, when you are obliged to concern yourself with something completely foreign to your interests, attention wavers, boredom blunts your senses and time drags endlessly.

Creative living means making the state of intense involvement a constant condition of our existence. That is the key to the conquest of time and the cornerstone to building a life of satisfaction and creative enjoyment.

To be sure, planning ahead and setting goals for the future are essential. But that activity is not to be confused with *living* in the future. Once we have decided on a goal, planned a course of action, we should, in a sense, *forget* the goal itself. Action—here and now—will move us toward it.

Most people are obsessed with the future. They idealize it, even in these troubled times, seeing it as bright and free from problems. But a trouble-free future cannot come merely from the passage of time; it can only result from creative activity *now*. It must be built on an accumulation of creative todays. As the psychiatrist Jacob List puts it, "The present is the only time we really have. Can we wait until tomorrow to live? Tomorrow does not exist. And having problems is no reason to postpone living. In fact, whenever possible, I say, 'Postpone the problems and make today pay off with something creative.' "

When we do something, then, let it be for the sake of the doing, for the experience. We should savor it in the present. We should try not to see our daily activities as a means to something else, something for the future, but as valuable in and of themselves.

Emotional Numbness

People in our culture rarely show their emotions. We instead tend to overemphasize the values of detachment, objectivity, logic, impersonality and "coolness." The deep-freezing of feelings and emotions, however, nips creativity in the bud.

That our culture has experienced a serious decline in accepting feeling as a normal part of life has been recognized by several perceptive writers, notably Robert Lynd. Lynd notes that,

> At point after point our culture plays down extensive, acute, and subtle feeling. To be "businesslike" is to be impersonal; in our moments of deep, personalized emotion we tend to retreat from others into ourselves or to the trusted tolerance of our immediate family; a businessman who is "artistic" may be somewhat suspect; being "romantic" or "idealistic" is regarded as an evidence of youth; and the person who "gets enthusiastic about things" is mildly disparaged as immature and "unsound." Human beings do not easily live so emotionally sterilized. So we burst out periodically in sex, drinking, hard-driving weekends, and gusts of safe, standardized feeling at the movies and football games.

Let's consider for a moment how vital feelings are in the creation of works of art. It almost seems that the intensity of feeling with which the artist works is largely responsible for the quality of what he produces. For example, Frank Howes points out that "in the various sorts of bad music, the crude, the rudimentary, the ephemeral . . . the prime cause of badness is *lack of heat* in the composer's imagination. Bad music is in fact underdone music, music not properly cooked by fire, but merely damped, smoked or warmed, music not wholly composed." Gertrude Stein remarked that "a book will come as deeply as it is felt, when it is running truest, and the book will never be truer or deeper than your feeling." D. H. Lawrence's observation is similar: "A picture lives with the life you put into it. If you put no life into it—no thrill, no concentration of delight or exaltation of visual discovery—then the picture is dead . . . no matter how much thorough and scientific work is put into it."

Added to this intensity of feeling in living and working has to be a specific personal involvement or attachment the creative individual feels toward everything connected with his work. The creative worker feels intense involvement with the medium he works with, whether it be words, sounds, colors, figures. This involvement does not, as a rule, happen suddenly or overnight, but begins early in the creative individual's career, and it is the surest sign that the individual possesses the necessary potential for a creative career.

PROBLEM SOLVING BLOCKS

Grabbing the First Idea

Most people, when faced with a problem, tend to grab the first solution that occurs to them and rest content with it. Rare, indeed, is the individual who keeps on trying to find other solutions to his problem. This is especially evident when a person feels under pressure, or when he experiences frustrations with a recalcitrant problem over a period of time.

Experience has shown, however, that the really effective ideas and solutions come when a quantity of alternatives has been generated. The really creative problem solver doesn't feel the need to clutch and run with the first notion, but can patiently wait for more unique and apt solutions that occur later on in the creative process.

Premature Judgments

Most individuals have a tendency to jump to conclusions and make premature judgments. And once a judgment is arrived at, we tend to persevere in it even when the evidence is overwhelming that we are wrong. Effective school teachers know the importance of teaching students to refrain from guessing prematurely at an explanation when searching for a principle underlying a situation or event. Once an explanation is articulated, it is difficult to revise or drop it in the face of contradictory evidence.

Many interesting psychological experiments have demonstrated the fixating power of premature judgments. In one experiment, color slides of familiar objects, such as a fire hydrant, were projected upon a screen and people were asked to try to identify the objects while they were still out of focus. Gradually, through several stages, the focus was improved. The striking finding was this: If an individual wrongly identified an object while it was far out of focus, he frequently still could not identify it correctly when it was brought sufficiently into focus so that another person who had not seen the blurred vision could easily identify it. What this indicates is that considerably more effort and evidence is necessary to overcome an incorrect judgment, hypothesis or belief than is required to establish a correct one. A person who is in the habit of jumping to conclusions frequently closes his mind to new information, and limited awareness hampers creative solutions.

Solution-mindedness

In his extensive studies on problem solving, psychologist Norman R. Maier discovered that most individuals, when they are confronted with a problem, feel strong internal pressure to find a solution—in short, they are excessively solution-minded. When they were encouraged—after they had achieved the first solution—to proceed further and seek a second solution, the second solution was invariably a more creative one. Maier concluded that this was because of a shift to problem orientation; the subjects were no longer driven to find a solution for they had already accomplished that task. Now they were relaxed, and free to turn the problem over on all sides and entertain different viewpoints. Maier found that this simple shift from solution-mindedness to problem-mindedness increased creative solutions from 16 percent to over 52 percent.

Overmotivation

There is little doubt that for effective creative performance, some high-octane motivational fuel is necessary. However, some people manage to blunt their effectiveness by either excessive motivation, or the desire to succeed too quickly and grandiosely.

Several adverse consequences result from overmotivation. First, the overmotivated person may misunderstand the real problem. He (or she) might overlook the obvious, or narrow his field of observation too much. He may look for and utilize only those clues that provide a quick solution to his problem, and be thus apt to pass up many things that could lead to a more novel or better solution. The overmotivated person frequently fails to consider a number of possible alternatives and will therefore latch on to the first one that seems at all workable.

Second, the overmotivated person frequently fails to be global, or generic, in his observations. He fails to see the relationship between the problem components and gives inadequate consideration to the basic attributes or ideas that surround the problem.

Overmotivation may also result in excessively ambitious goals. Some individuals live in a state of perpetual frustration and disappointment because they want to tackle only very big, very recalcitrant and very complex projects, pitched unrealistically beyond their capabilities.

Incessant Effort

Some individuals tend to tackle problems with dogged, incessant effort. Although highly commendable if it enhances one's analytical grasp of a problem, the tendency to keep busy without time out for relaxation and for change of activity can frequently serve as an effective barrier to the emergence of novel solutions to problems.

The person who knows when persistence with a recalcitrant problem begins to bring diminishing returns and who then drops it for a while, frequently finds that, upon returning to the problem, a new approach comes with greater ease.

Concrete- or Practical-mindedness

This straight-to-the-point type of block insists that instead of roaming imaginatively around a problem, we get down to the facts immediately. It is shortsighted to zero in on an early definition of a problem because it precludes consideration of the broader scope inherent in almost any problem situation. "Premature particularization," says William J. J. Gordon, "is very often a symptom of an individual's concern with being impractical."

A. L. Simberg of General Motors has also noted how trigger-ready some individuals are to invoke practical and economical judgment when imagination should be given free rein. He illustrates this with the following example:

> Our chief engineer gives us the assignment of developing a new product. He tells us that he wants something that is really practical but yet it must be startlingly different. Unfortunately . . . at the sound of the word "practical," our imaginations cease to function. Would it not be just as simple to start with the "startlingly different" idea and engineer this back to practicality? Learn to try to shoot for the single great idea at the outset. Take your chance on the one-in-a-million shot. You can always come back to reality by stages.

In spite of some improvements in the quality of our organizational life-styles, people still tend to feel slightly guilty if they enjoy what they're doing, if they fail to produce as fast as their colleagues, or if they feel that what they're contributing is not of immediate practical value or is too far from facts.

Intolerance of Complexity

A person who wants to be a creative problem solver should be able to tolerate a high degree of complexity. He has to perceive a great variety of possibilities, and be able to consider and balance different or even contradictory frames of reference, concepts, elements, etc., without prematurely discarding those that do not permit easy comprehension and categorization. Often, when difficulty is experienced in maintaining an open flow of relationships or multiple possible relationships simultaneously, the tendency is to "run away," that is, to "close out" the problem by accepting a simple or stereotyped solution.

Habit Transfer

One very common obstacle to creative problem solving is the past conditioning of our thoughts and actions. When this happens, we attack new problems only with methods and procedures that have proved successful before, rather than trying new, untried approaches that might have greater potential for successfully solving the problem at hand.

Individuals with strong analytical ability and ego-involvement with previous successes are prone to have this block. Although they are fully able to reduce the new problem to its fundamentals, they may feel afraid that any new creative synthesis may not "live up" to their past performances.

A person can become more aware of this tendency to habit transfer if he occasionally asks himself these questions:

"Did the problem seem so familiar that I tossed off a solution based on previously successful approaches, rather than investigating other avenues of approach?"

"If I relied solely on a past approach, was it out of a considered decision that this was the best approach, or was it to avoid the effort and insecurity that a new approach might entail?"

"Has familiarity with an area caused me to seize upon a few basic approaches to the extent that I may fail to recognize situations in which they do not apply?"

Inability to Suspend Critical Judgment

Because of the concrete and practical background provided by our education and general experience, most of us are fearful of the disorderly state of mind and incipient confused excitement that creative activity engenders. In order to move with concentration, energy and courage toward a goal, we feel in need of a minutely defined purpose—a detailed blueprint. Thus, when engaged in creative problem solving, there is a tendency to judge or evaluate our own ideas before they are fully formed, often robbing the virgin idea of the value and validity with which it should be viewed at the moment it first occurs.

During the heat of creative shaping and forming of an idea, we must be able to submerge ourselves in the creative current. We must give ourselves up to this experience and be keenly—almost exclusively—aware only of the suggestions that emerge from the subconscious. At such a time, consciousness of the familiar sort should be blotted out so that the emerging aspects of the new idea can pass through our minds in whatever forms they may take: fragments of associations, images, broken or incomplete sentences. At this stage, we should "feel" our idea rather than "think" it. No single item should be pinpointed for attention so that the full range of unconscious activity can have free play.

The acceptance and commitment of ideas as they emerge while one is working on a problem is a very delicate affair. To maintain uninterrupted rapport with the unconscious, the temptation to criticize or weigh each articulated fragment must be resisted. According to many creative persons, nothing so stifles the creative process as critical judgment applied too early to the emerging idea.

This does not mean that criticism, judgment and evaluation have no place in the production of new ideas. On the contrary, they serve a vital purpose. But premature weighing of "bits and pieces" of an idea as these come forth should be avoided. In effect, during the birth of an idea critical judgment should be suspended.

More half-finished ideas have hit the wastebasket because of their creator's own evaluative attitude and distrust of tenuous suggestions emerging from his or her mind than for any inherent weakness or absurdity in the idea itself. Much time has been lost, too, through the too early critical weighing and rejection of an idea that is later retrieved and followed up.

The following rule about creativity should be, therefore, laid down with considerable emphasis: The longer one can linger with an idea, with judgment held in abeyance, the longer one can "feel" the idea with all its ramifications and virtually "soak" in it, the better the chance of exploiting it fully.

Poor Problem Solving Approaches

The myriad blocks to correct problem solving approaches include the following:

- Incorrect problem definition or statement.
- Difficulty in isolating the real problem.
- Seeing only a narrow aspect of a problem situation.
- Being misled by either inadequate clues or misleading information.
- Being overwhelmed by the immensity or scope of the problem.
- Remaining within the obvious boundaries of a problem.

Correct problem definition or statement is crucial to arriving at effective creative solutions. Incorrect problem definition ties the individual down to a restrictive error and hampers flexibility and fluency of thought. Consequently, the first problem definitions should be considered tentative. Occasionally further data must be first collected to define the problem at all. Here are some do's and don'ts you should observe in your problem solving approach:

Defining the Problem

DO'S

State your problem in a simple, basic, broad, generic way, so that the statement does not limit or confine your thinking.

Look beyond the immediate problem to its fundamentals. If necessary, search in literature to marshal a better understanding of the many ramifications that might be pertinent to your problem's solution.

See if you can't state your problem in a different way. Remember that unlike analytical problems, which have only one right answer, creative problems have several acceptable or right solutions. A listing of variations on problem statement may even suggest the idea for solution.

Keep asking yourself: "What are the actual boundaries of the problem?" "What are the unusual aspects of the problem?" "What are the commonest aspects of the problem, those that

DON'TS

Don't structure your problem statement too much.

Don't load your problem statement with the side problems or conditions. Strip from it as many modifying adjectives, adverbs and phrases as possible.

Don't suggest a solution in your problem definition.

Don't fail to keep in your mind's eye the total situation and the proper relationship of the parts in the whole.

DO'S   DON'TS

everybody takes for granted, and can they really be taken for granted?"

Break down the parameters or variables of the problem through analysis.

After the Problem Is Defined

DO'S

Prepare yourself a problem sheet on which you write down your problem statement(s).

List the ideas and various approaches you feel might conceivably solve the problem. Take off in different directions and amass as many leads as you can. Note down all the ideas, even the insignificant ones, but abstain from dwelling on any single one of them too long. Many of the fleeting thoughts that in isolation may look to you inconsequential may contain a new vital germ of an idea, or later, combine with other thoughts into a new, meaningful idea.

Exhaust all the possible and conceivable hypotheses and plans of action. Consider even the most unlikely solutions. List the many specific methods that you could use to approach the problem solution. Ask yourself apparently irrelevant questions.

DON'TS

Remember that no idea should be rejected as of no consequence until so proven. Don't follow one line of thought at this point, for this would prevent others from occurring. Even if you feel that you have hit upon one idea that seems to you to be the best answer to your problem, resist the impulse to stop the process. You have it written down and it won't be lost.

Don't refer to any great extent to the literature for data when the creative current runs strong. Cursory checking on facts is all right, but extensive literature searches at this time can divert you completely from your original line of thought.

Don't evaluate any of the suggestions and hunches that occur to you at this time.

Don't fail to distinguish between cause and effect and relate the

DO'S

Look for analogous situations in other areas, at the same time remembering that none will fit your problem precisely.

Relax your binding faith in reason and logic when thinking up ideas and let your imagination soar. Learn to let yourself and your imagination go.

Have faith in yourself and believe that the answer will come.

DON'TS

problem to its environment. Examine the conditions and relationships of your problem from the framework of all the possible solutions you have listed.

Don't be put down by failure. Continue working at your problem even in the face of serious discouragement and resist the temptation to give up.

Don't be disturbed if you experience a sense of stress when looking for a solution. Without the feeling of pressure and need, you run the risk of not finding the best solution.

Sustained creative thinking, when the problem is tackled from every conceivable angle, will usually yield enough material for you to put it into a systematic, orderly outline. Frequently, to your surprise, you may have come up with many more ideas than you thought you would be capable of. Even if no satisfactory solution emerges, this unremitting, sustained creative thinking will leave your unconscious with a wealth of material to work on, and after a few days away from the problem, upon renewing creative thinking, you may find that you are more productive than during your previous session. The next time you tackle your problem, go over the ideas you had listed previously. Try various combinations of them. Often one idea will start you off in a completely new direction. This time follow it freely, even though it may seem to you that the new train of thought takes you away from your immediate concern or problem area.

If you still do not make any progress toward a solution, reexamine your problem with reference to the problem definition(s): Is it too broad, preventing anchorage points? Is it too limited, narrowing your field of thought? Should you divide your problem into several subproblems and work on them one at a time? In any case, the previous efforts at analysis and definition have given you a better understanding of your problem, and now after you have redefined it, you may be on the last lap of a determined surge toward the solution.

Lack of Disciplined Effort

Absence of consistent and purposive effort can act as a barrier to creative performance. The three most common causes are: demotivation, self-aggrandizement and idle fantasy.

A person is usually demotivated when he has to *force* himself to do the task at hand, when he lacks proper or sufficient stimulation to produce creatively, or when the pictured goal is subjectively seen as not worth hard work and self-disciplined application. A clearer sense of personal identity can be obtained through periodic examination of one's personal values, potentialities, temperament and needs. A crystallized conception of what one is and wants goes a long way toward promoting greater purposive striving.

Self-aggrandizement usually makes us overestimate the talents, knowledge and skills we possess. When actual performance does not match our inflated aspirations, we tend to lapse into lassitude, or blame others for their obtuseness and lack of appreciation of our "genius." A balanced appraisal of one's assets, as well as limitations, contributes greatly toward self-knowledge and estimation of one's true potentials.

Idle fantasy conjures up the attainment of desired goals without the necessary toil, effort and discipline that would be required to actualize them in reality. There are individuals who habitually turn their wishes of accomplishment into fantasy and cannot bring themselves to face the arduous road ahead for actualizing the pictured successes.

ENVIRONMENTAL-ORGANIZATIONAL BLOCKS

Clinging to the Established

Time-tested methods, standard procedures, policies, rules and regulations give many individuals a feeling of anchorage and security. The clearly defined, the firmly established, the things that make their world secure and predictable, have a powerful hold on them. A proposed new idea thus frequently appears as a direct threat to their sense of security. "After all," the reasoning goes, "why should we disturb things as they are when they seem to be working well?"

There is also a feeling that accepting a new idea may denigrate the worth or validity of what already exists. Or the reasoning goes, "We have enough problems as is; why add problems we might not be able to cope with?" Clearly, accepting change, which new ideas inevitably brings about, means more headaches, work and responsibility.

Nevertheless companies do exist that encourage new ideas and bold creative advances and thus move ahead by leaps and bounds. It has been observed that businesses whose managements fear innovation, develop into copiers, or seek only relatively small, predictable and orderly improvements. The danger inherent in this unrealistic caution and the tendency to cling to the familiar is that it may stunt the creative growth of the organization to a degree where it fails to adequately cope with competition.

And isn't it rather strange that Polaroid film was not invented by Kodak, that hand-held calculators were not invented by IBM, that digital watches were not invented by the watchmakers?

Resistance to New Ideas

The image that most of us have of ourselves is that we are not only open-minded and willing to consider new ideas and thoughts, but encouraging and supportive of them. Experience, however, has indicated that this attitude is seldom demonstrated in practice.

George M. Prince, who studied thousands of tape recordings of idea-presentation sessions, feels that our natural reaction to new ideas is to look for the disadvantages in them, rather than at their benefits. As he points out,

> Each of us pays convincing lip service to his willingness—even eagerness—to consider new thoughts and ideas. But a thousand tapes, such as we have made, make liars of us all. People use remarkable ingenuity to make clear by tone, nonverbal slights, tuning out, helpful criticism, false issues, and outright negativity that they are not only against ideas and change, but also against those who propose it. We humans habitually try to protect ourselves even from our own new ideas.

The most common resistance to new ideas stems from people's resistance to change. Everyone knows even routine changes in organizations create resistance. It is easy to imagine how much resistance a radically new idea creates. Whoever said, "Creation is a stone thrown uphill against the downward rush of habit," did not exaggerate.

Any organization that wishes to survive has to have rules, regulations and controls to channel the actions and behavior of its individual members into a predictable and orderly routine. Without planned and predictable routine the organization would lapse into chaos. Thus, a certain amount of *inflexibility* is necessary to accomplish organizational objectives.

Creative ideas and innovation, which upset organizational order and routine, are therefore often regarded with inhospitable and intolerant attitudes. Yet, without creativity and innovation, organizations could not stay viable and prosperous for long. It is for these reasons that there is such a perennial ambivalence toward new ideas. Unfortunately, many organizations, especially the larger ones, become overburdened with formal and informal rules to a degree where any hope for real creativity is almost completely snuffed out and conformity rules the day.

One way or another, there has always been a resistance to accepting new ideas. Even as successful an inventor as Thomas Alva Edison stated: "Society is never prepared to receive any inventions. Every new thing is resisted, and it takes years for the inventor to get people to listen to him before it can be introduced."

When we review the resistance people have shown toward innovations in the arts, or toward discoveries and inventions, the documented stories seem almost unbelievable.

For example, when the Impressionists first exhibited their works in Paris, they met with storms of abuse and scorn. Similarly, when Ibsen's plays were first produced in England, they incurred hostile and curiously irrational criticism. Clement Scott wrote of *A Doll's House*: "The atmosphere is hideous . . . it is all self, self, self "; *The Standard* called the play "morbid and unwholesome"; and *The People* labeled it "unnatural and immoral."

The performance of Stravinsky's *Le Sacre du Printemps* by the Russian Ballet in Paris in May 1913 created a scandalous pandemonium. Most of the audience had such a poor understanding of Stravinsky's genius that they seriously believed he was cynically hell-bent to destroy music as an art form, and the performance was halted by catcalls and abuse.

Railroads, when they were first introduced, were regarded by many as useless, and farmers raised a protest against them, claiming that the noise the trains would make would frighten their cattle from grazing and their hens from laying eggs. Even such distinguished men as Daniel Webster and Ruskin objected to railroads.

The automobile was first regarded as a devil-inspired device, and an argument was raised before the British Association for the Advancement of Science that the horseless carriage would fail because the human driver "has not the advantage of the intelligence of the horse in shaping his path."

The printing press was another invention that evoked strong resistance. Not only did the calligraphers, whose craft was threatened with extinction, malign the new device, but also those who feared the social consequences if the masses learned to read. In 1671, the Governor of Virginia put forth his official opinion: "I thank God we have no free schools nor printing; and I hope we shall not have these for a hundred years. For learning has brought disobedience and heresy and sects into the world; and printing has divulged them and libels against the government. God keep us from both." Similar reactions were shown toward the telegraph, the airplane, the incandescent lamp, the typewriter. Even the common bathtub, when it was first introduced into the United States, was described as "an epicurean innovation" from England designed to corrupt the democratic simplicity of the Republic. When President Fillmore had a bathtub installed in the White House in 1851, he was vilified and charged with the crime of "monarchical luxury."

The history of creativity and innovation show that the creative people who emerged throughout the centuries were endowed with a creative drive of such determination and strength that it enabled them to withstand ridicule and suppression, the demand for conformity and the financial deprivation to which they were subjected. No one knows, of course, how many other equally talented individuals, the "mute inglorious Miltons" who were deficient in motivation and drive, succumbed to the overwhelming societal resistance and pressures.

In fairness, however, it should be pointed out that there are sometimes valid and compelling reasons for the rejection of new ideas.

Occasionally the sheer number of ongoing projects, or the list of priorities is so crowded that undertaking work on the new ideas might disrupt the work the company is already committed to accomplish. In this case a person should consider his or her idea as one whose time has not yet come, and it should be held in abeyance until a more propitious occasion.

A new idea sometimes bears a striking resemblance to an idea that was previously submitted by somebody else, and frequently the individual is not aware of the fact that an idea he has worked long and hard on is already being implemented. This, however, should not disappoint the originator unduly, for it is a clear proof that he can produce practical ideas and may, in the future, come up with something entirely new.

Occasionally a good idea would be so costly to develop that it would be impracticable to undertake from the company's standpoint. Simple economics in most companies dictates what can and what cannot be developed.

Sometimes a new idea involves only a small part of a procedure, process or product that is scheduled for a complete change. The proposed partial idea may not fit in with the planned overall change.

There are also occasionally quite legitimate reasons why a person should refrain from putting in the extra time and effort involved in developing a presentation for his idea. His regular duties might be such that he has little time to devote to the task. Or his idea might be in an area where his background knowledge is inadequate, or existing information that would buttress his sales argument is either incomplete or unavailable. Why risk one's good reputation for sound judgment by being forced to admit this publicly?

A person might also be uncertain as to the probable value, practicality, or timeliness of his idea. While many of these considerations might be convenient rationalizations to escape extra work and effort, in individual cases and in certain organizations they are perfectly legitimate.

It should be remembered that even if ideas do not always get accepted, the practice of creative ideation has other commendable benefits. Creative thinking prevents one from going stale on one's job; it enhances understanding of one's work; it is a stimulating mental exercise and invaluable for self-development.

Creative problem solving can be profitably used in all areas of living. The individual who after a few rebuffs resolves never to propose another idea, may hurt his organization, but he surely hurts himself most.

Smugnosis

Smugnosis is an affliction that affects judgment adversely. It propels the individual to arrive at negative conclusions, based on the omniscient trust he has in his own information and knowledge. Individuals with advanced formal education and degrees are particularly susceptible to smugnosis.

Only a few years before the first atomic explosion, an internationally respected scientist and authority on atomic energy publicly stated that a millennium of research and developmental effort would be required to produce an atomic bomb. After it became a reality, an equally famous scientist stated that the odds were a hundred to one against the development of a hydrogen bomb.

Both the rapid change dynamics of the present and the spreading disease of smugnosis prompted the writer Elbert Hubbard to come up with the following very apt observation: "The world is moving so fast these days that the man who says it can't be done is generally interrupted by someone doing it."

Threat to Security and Status

Some people react negatively to a new idea because it is not their own. Many managers and supervisors are especially prone to play down the value of new ideas because they feel that their power and status are threatened if their underlings or even their associates suggest them. They feel that if changes should be instituted, then they should have thought of them in the first place. They resist ideas because they were not the first to think of them.

Change is also frequently fought because it makes someone's job insecure, or tumbles an expert from his pinnacle. For example, a technical innovation may introduce a completely new approach to the way in which a particular job is tackled. A person who for years has followed a particular practice with great skill and confidence, may suddenly find himself a novice who is feeling his way, starting the slow, painful path of learning a new skill.

Innovative change may undermine individuals' security in ways other than loss of status or skill. It may also be perceived as a direct threat to their earnings, position, chance for advancement, recognition and favorable working conditions.

Transgression into Private Domains

Some people feel that new ideas, especially when they originate in another department of the company, encroach on their rightful province. Each person's responsibility in an organization is, as a rule, carefully defined, and people come to regard these responsibilities as their private preserves. When somebody comes up with an idea that concerns some other person's area, the usual reaction is defensiveness and/or hostility, for the person tends to feel that nobody else has the right to trespass into his area of specialization.

This artificial, but very real barrier, not only kills a lot of valuable ideas, but it prevents the communication and free flow of information that should exist between different departments. Lucius D. Clay shocked many people some years ago when he asserted that the person on his staff who "got ahead" was the one who, seeing an unmet need or an unsolved problem, took it on himself or herself to do something about it no matter in whose province it technically belonged. He knew the implications of fearing to transgress organizational lines because of "proprietary rights."

The delightful and penetrating researches of Robert Ardrey in his books *African Genesis* and *The Territorial Imperative* are particularly fitting and relevant here. He discovered that the wolf will urinate in a circle and the hippopotamus will defecate around his domain to establish territorial claims. Figuratively speaking, at least, aren't many of our hippopotami-managers and wolflike employees following suit?

Dependency Feelings

With the increasing complexity of modern society, the network of our mutual dependencies is increasing. Yet, these dependencies are frequently the enemies of creativity.

Let's examine briefly how dependency expectations operate in our business and industrial environments. The typical employee usually defers responsibility and control to those actually assigned the responsibility for tasks and projects; he rarely takes charge of his own actions. He waits for direction, stimulation and approval and tends to rely on the opinions and judgment of others rather than cultivate his own evaluation. He is encouraged and challenged, not to be an independently creative person, but a passive, dependently adaptive individual who must use his energy and his mind to please individuals who are higher in the organizational pecking order. He feels he must suppress his creative individuality in order to keep in line with the multiple group-belongings necessary for keeping his job and supporting his organizational identity.

Dependency is also reinforced through the fear of failure. The degree of individual responsibility for failure is considerably lessened if an idea and its subsequent implementation have been approved and decided upon "in a committee," and if the individual can claim immunity through not having acted independently. The temptation, in the face of failure, to ease one's ego by saying "it was his idea," exists in most of us. By the same token, we often accept and use ideas and methods we know are inferior to our own in order to be able to "share the blame" should things go wrong.

No Time for Creative Thinking

Most of us who work in organizations are constantly interrupted by telephone calls, urgent memos, visits by colleagues, idle chatter, unscheduled meetings, letter-writing and a whole host of "administrivia" that leave little time for creative thinking. One effective way of overcoming this is to define and redefine one's primary functions so that time is reserved for creativity.

Ronald Clark reports that Albert Einstein used to receive enormous amounts of correspondence. This included just plain fan mail and all sorts of requests for Einstein to lecture, make appearances, support causes, loan money and write letters of recommendation. When Einstein was deeply involved in working on the General Theory of Relativity he needed to work alone and undisturbed much of the time. How did he handle this flood of correspondence? Einstein kept a big meat hook hanging from the ceiling above his desk, and when he was particularly occupied, he would simply hang whole packages of unopened letters on the hook for future attention. A visitor, noticing huge bundles on the hook asked him what he did when the meat hook was full. Einstein answered with a simple, "Burn 'em!"

Whether we can really follow Einstein's example in a corporate setup is a moot question. What it implies, however, is that we have more leeway than we think when choosing the way we respond and react to outside expectations and demands. In addition, setting of priorities and other time-management techniques enable you to reserve solid blocks of uninterrupted time for creative thinking.

Competition vs. Cooperation

Paradoxically, both competition and cooperation, usually considered to be polar opposites, can inhibit creativity. An overemphasis on cooperation frequently means that the individual must inhibit or temper his initiative, resources and creative ideas to "fit in," or sometimes even to keep his job. Overemphasis on competition usually involves win-lose dynamics. The individual feels that he is working against someone else and only one person can succeed. With this attitude the quality of solutions to problems, or the excellence of the product to be created, becomes of secondary importance.

Of the two, cooperation and competition, the latter is more crippling of creativity and more ingrained in our organizational value systems. As psychologist A. R. Wight puts it,

> Our society is so imbued with the spirit of competition, and so convinced of its merit, that eliminating the win-at-any-cost competition from an individual's repertoire of values, attitudes, and behavior becomes a major undertaking. The attitude that competition is "good" is generalized to include all competition, or it is argued that man is by nature competitive, that competition is instinctive. But most human behavior is learned behavior, and competition is taught, valued, and rewarded in our society. . . . It is quite possible that this emphasis on winning is associated with or contributes to the development of desire for power, status, and prestige, which also interfere with creative group performance. These personal ob-

jectives take precedence over organizational objectives in any situation, and politics and infighting become the rule.

Lack of Interest in Problems

Most of us working in organizational or corporate setups spend most of our time working on problems dictated by the needs and requirements of the organization. This often means that we are called upon to tackle problems that do not hold any particular interest for us—with consequent reduction in creative performance. Psychologist Richard N. Wallen explains it this way:

> One serious block occurs when we are pushed to solve a problem that doesn't concern us. When we are fascinated, we feel the problem pulling us. We do not feel pushed into it. The fascinating problem is one that we choose, that somehow belongs to us. People do not need to be driven to do things that have an intrinsic attraction. . . . I do not believe that people can be pushed into being creative. Faced with a demand for a solution to a problem they have not chosen, people may come up with ideas. I do not think that they reach their best creative thinking under such conditions.

Fantasy Making Is Worthless

Daydreaming, reverie, speculative meanderings have always been the forerunners of new creative works. Most creative products were at one time merely the musings and fantasies of an actively receptive, imaginatively far-ranging mind. Our culture, however, discourages daydreaming. It is still widely regarded not only as a waste of time, but as indicative of lack of maturity, if not of serious psychopathology.

In most of our business organizations, the individuals who are physically active paper shufflers, who move around, pace the corridors and visit with their colleagues, are considered valuable. On the other hand, the employee who quietly sits and thinks at his desk and occasionally stares into space, is considered suspect or lazy. Because of the organizational insistence on looking busy all the time, the person who tries to do some creative thinking feels uncomfortable and guilty, particularly if the boss happens to survey the scene. This is only one of the ways in which business atmosphere discourages creative ideation.

Busy-ness

Most of us seem to equate busy-ness with effectiveness; we feel uneasy or guilty if we are not constantly doing something. Even in our hobbies, play and recreation, the deadly serious pursuit of a specific goal or practical accomplishment frequently mars the pleasure we ought to derive from what essentially should be pure relaxation for recharging the creative batteries.

How harmful our preoccupation with "constructive activity" really is, can be illustrated by the very prevalent "retirement neurosis" in our culture. Unused to creative leisure and playfulness, upon retirement a great many men and women suddenly find themselves confronting painful, unbearable boredom. This results in feelings of deep depression and often in a rapid deterioration of their psychological as well as their physical health.

Hyperactivity is in reality an empty affair and it has contributed to our general restlessness and our inability to receptively concentrate on any one thing for any length of time. Erich Fromm has well described how hyperactivity actually amounts to doing nothing. As he says,

> We are always busy, but without concentration. When we do one thing, we are already thinking of the next thing, of the moment when we can stop doing what we are doing now. . . . We do, if possible, many things at the same time. We eat breakfast, listen to the radio, and read the newspaper, and perhaps at the same time we carry on a conversation with

our wife and children. We do five things at the same time, and we do nothing. . . . If one is truly concentrated, the very thing one is doing at this moment is the most important thing in life. If I talk to someone, if I read something, if I walk— whatever it is, if I do it in a concentrated fashion, there is nothing more important than what I am doing in the here and now.

Isolation of the Creative Person

Creativity feeds on the stimulation-sharing and cross-fertilization of ideas that a congenial group of like-minded individuals can provide. In many organizations, unfortunately, such channels for creativity-stimulating experiences are lacking. This was expressed with lucid directness by one creative specialist in a medium-size organization:

> We have many specialists in our organization. I happen to be one of these. Each of us can understand things from his particular angle; all the others understand things from their particular angles. When I get a bright idea, there is no one to whom I can go and be really understood. What's creative to me is not seen as creative by anyone else because they don't have the background to know what I had to do to get to where I got; they can't see what's new about it. In these circumstances, it's easy to lose interest in creating simply because you can't really share it. There's probably a lot of creativity in our organization we can't ever see because we individually don't know enough to recognize it.

Fear That Ideas Will Be Stolen

There are individuals who feel they will have only a few good ideas which they must jealously guard, or they might be stolen. While this occasionally can be a realistic fear, there are a multitude of ways to safeguard against it. Affixing one's signature on a written-out idea and then circulating it among several people, is frequently sufficient for protecting ownership.

Creative people behave in a different fashion. They act as if their supply of ideas is endless, and for them it usually is. They don't have to waste time and energy protecting one idea. Rather, they use their energies for producing more. Not only can ideas be smothered to death by overprotection, but a suspicious and overcautious attitude may even seriously inhibit one's power to produce them.

Risky Road of Organizational Channels

Before the further development of an idea is approved, it frequently has to travel through layers and layers of supervisors and decision makers. That this poses a real risk to the idea has been pointed out by numerous creative individuals. One of them expressed it this way:

Suppose I get an idea I want to explore. It isn't ready to be put into formal shape. I just want to clear it as an idea and to find out whether individuals up the line in the organization would support it. First I talk with my group leader. Let's suppose he and I get along well; our minds and personalities click. He takes the idea to the section head. The group leader and the section head make up a new pair for doing business around this area. I like my group leader because I'm confident he doesn't change into another sort of person when he enters this new situation, but both he and I know there is a long gauntlet ahead where there can be a break in the pairs. From section chief, a new pair is formed with the department supervisor, then between the supervisor and department director, then between the department director and the technical director, and then between the technical director and the division manager. This is just inside our division on the way up—six pairs! The idea might involve still more pairs beyond that and then again more pairs on the way down, if the idea was the kind that would involve other divisions of the company. A break anywhere along the line could be critical. My idea could get distorted all out of shape or lost altogether since it is not worked out in its ramifications and is easily subject to attack. It can become a scapegoat for most anything. Given these circumstances, you can see I'm not going to be spouting ideas very often.

Inability to Enlist Involvement

It often happens that even when we've solved a tough problem, or come up with a good idea, nobody seems interested. Sometimes this is due to a lack of confidence in the merits of our idea, but most often this puzzling indifference relates to our failure to get others involved.

Idea implementation requires cooperative, mutual effort. Too many ideas have remained undeveloped because the originator was too ego-centered, too stubbornly possessive, or aggressively resistant to any suggested modifications or improvements. He thus fails to elicit the participation and cooperation of his associates in the developmental stages of his idea.

Some idea originators are so ego-involved with their ideas that any suggestions of improvement or modification are resisted out of hand as unnecessary tamperings with their brainchildren. Actually, suggestions for improvement should be heartily welcomed. When others take a keen interest in your idea, they become personally involved, and your idea is transformed into "our idea." Be generous in sharing credit with others; everyone will be a winner and you will be remembered as the one who came up with the original concept in the first place.

If you hug your idea to your bosom too strongly, others will not come to your aid when you meet obstacles. It is the shortest route to resentment and negative reactions.

Even if somebody suggests revisions that, to your mind, would add very little or almost nothing meaningful to your idea, you would still be ill advised to reject them. For if you force others to accept your idea without the suggested revisions, they might later—during the implementation stage—drag their feet, or outright sabotage it.

If at all possible, try to build up an atmosphere of mutuality, and make others feel they are participants, or co-creators of your idea, rather than passive listeners who must sit in judgment. The "we-approach" rather than the "I-approach" has been the most important ingredient in many successful idea-sales situations.

The following excellent checklist designed to enlist others' involvement was developed by Joel Weston, Jr., president of Hanes Dye and Finishing Company of North Carolina.

WHO? . . . WHY? . . . HOW? . . . WHAT? . . . WHEN? . . . WHERE?

Who?
Who might be involved? What group?

Who might make contributions to the achievement desired?

Who might be favorably placed, and who might have special talents or resources to help?

What special strengths, capabilities or resources might they contribute?

What favorable circumstances might they be suitably placed to exploit?

Who might I need to convince of the value of the idea to be implemented?

In what ways, where and when, might they help?

What other ideas or challenges have you found by answering these "who?" questions?

Why?
Why might they freely or willingly lend their support?

What ways might you and/or others gain or benefit from this implementation?

What challenges or opportunities for expressing talents might be provided?

What might lead them to volunteer their services?

What might gain enthusiasm for the idea?

What opportunities might be provided for them or for you to excel or to shine?

In what ways might their participation further their own interests?

What might gain their or your acceptance?

What might gain support for your aims and activities?

How might you demonstrate, dramatize, visualize the benefits?

What other ideas or challenges have you found by answering the "why?" questions?

How? How might you or others be rewarded for supporting the idea?

How might you pretest the idea?

How might you translate your idea into practice?

How might you insure its effectiveness?

How might continual or progressive feedback and corrective action be provided?

What might be a possible method for achieving your aims?

What steps might be necessary?

What might be a possible plan of action?

What provisions might be necessary to anticipate and overcome difficulties, obstacles, constraints, limitations, objections?

In what ways might critical factors or people be controlled?

What other ideas or challenges have you found by answering the "how?" questions?

What? What resources might help you to take the necessary steps and to make sure that you succeed? (Materials, equipment, finances, time, authority, permission, licenses, etc.)

Who might provide these needs?

When might they be provided?

Where might they be provided?

How might they be provided?

What new challenges might the idea pose?

How might you anticipate and meet these new challenges?

How might the idea be improved before it is used in implementation?

What other ideas or challenges have you found by answering the "what?" questions?

When?   When might the idea be completed?

What timing might be used?

What might be a suitable schedule, or action calender for necessary steps and events in the implementation?

What special days or dates might be helpful in reinforcing your strategy for putting the idea into action?

What other ideas or challenges have you found by answering the "when?" questions?

Where?   Where might you begin for maximum, quick, visible progress?

What special places, locations, circumstances, occasions, times, days, or approaches might be utilized for reestablishing and insuring self-generating momentum?

What might be a very first step?

What other ideas or challenges have you found by answering the "where?" questions?

OTHER BLOCKS AND BARRIERS

- Accepting the idea that the problem is too difficult and beyond one's understanding.
- Superficiality—shallowness, incompleteness and hastiness in thinking and problem solving.
- Judging too quickly.
- Failure to acquire sufficient information to solve a problem.
- Failure to relate the problem to its environment.
- Inability to see the problem from various viewpoints.
- Inflexible use of problem solving strategies.
- Belief that humor is out of place in problem solving.
- Inability to abandon an unworkable approach.
- Language skills too poor to record or express ideas.
- Failure to distinguish between cause and effect.
- Too much faith in statistics.
- Difficulty in seeing remote relationships.
- Failure to use all the senses in observing.
- Belief that it is not wise to doubt or to question.
- Belief that to be inquisitive is to be impolite.
- Imitation of the behavior patterns of others.
- Fear of asking questions that show ignorance.
- Undue concern with the opinions of others.
- Freezing of behavior into rigid patterns.
- Excessive involvement with others and neglect of own needs.
- Fear of being a pioneer, or "first" in a field.
- Excessive desire or preoccupation with security.

- Fear of exploring the unknown.
- Excessive dependence on authorities.
- Negativity toward the new and novel.
- Attitude of "play it safe."
- Lack of initiative, or "self-starting" ability.
- Fear that one's ideas will be stolen.
- Deeply rooted internal prejudices, biases and superstitions.
- Laziness—general lack of drive, incentives, ambition.
- Lack of self-awareness and self-orientation.
- Lack of spontaneity—inability to let capacities flow of themselves.
- Rigid defenses, inhibitions and fears.
- Narrow, truncated interests.
- Poor health—physiological and psychological problems—illness, tension, pain, anxiety, etc.
- Inability to relax.
- Boredom, passivity, chronic fatigue.
- Inability to distinguish reality from fantasy.
- Lack of appreciation of the value of imagination, fantasy, humor, dreaming; inability to open-mindedly tune in to "messages from within."

Boundaries are impinging on us. Only the
creative frontiers of the mind remain.
WILLIAM J. J. GORDON

The empires of the future are the empires
of the mind.
WINSTON CHURCHILL

The man with a new idea is a crank until
the idea succeeds.
MARK TWAIN

PART III

Characteristics of the Creative Individual

THE CREATIVE INDIVIDUAL has many distinct attributes or characteristics by which he or she can be identified and that significantly differentiate him from those who are less creative.

The kind and degree of creativity varies, of course, from person to person, and it is unlikely that any individual could possess all of the characteristics to a uniformly high degree. Rather, the descriptions that follow should be conceived as a composite profile of the "ideal" creative individual.

What is the value of gaining an insight into these characteristics? First, studying them closely will enable you to find your creative self described here and there and thus reinforce the attributes you already possess. Second, you will be able to uncover and pinpoint those attributes and abilities you feel you do not possess to a sufficient degree at present. Consciously cultivating these would substantially improve your creative performance. Thus, an assortment of exercises are included in this section to help you develop your unused potential. Finally, these new understandings and insights will enable you to create the means and conditions that can enhance your own internal powers and processes of creativity.

> *To conceive ideas is exhilarating, but it is only safe when you conceive so many that you ascribe no undue consequence to them and can take them for what they are worth. People who conceive few find it very difficult not to regard them with inordinate respect.*
> W. SOMERSET MAUGHAM

Fluency

The two crucially vital attributes for creative problem solving are *fluency* and *flexibility*.

The creative individual has the ability to generate and juggle a large number of ideas when confronting a problem or seeking improvements. He can scan more alternative thoughts, ride the wave of different associative currents and think of more ideas in a given span of time than do persons who are less creative. Capable of tapping his tropical imagination to scattershoot possibilities in volume, he stands a better chance of eventually selecting and developing the significant ideas.

Fluency can be demonstrated by a simple test, first developed by psychologist J. P. Guilford. One can ask people to list as many uses as they can think of for some common object, such as, for example, a red brick. If the person lists a large number of uses all in one class or category, such as construction or adornment, he shows fluency. If he, in addition, lists a number of uses that range over several categories (there are over sixteen such categories in the case of the red brick), he shows that he has, not only fluency, but also flexibility.

It must be pointed out that fluency of ideas and spontaneous expressiveness can be considerably enhanced if one learns to deliberately restrain or suppress critical judgment and evaluation of ideas as they occur—until one has marshaled all the ideas one is capable of coming up with. An overdeveloped or too-early critical attitude during the creative process can thoroughly inhibit fluency and the forward propulsion of ideas.

While there is little doubt that a person who wants to increase his creativity in problem solving should be willing to try, so to speak, a wide variety of wild shots in the dark and list a wealth of notions and ideas, it must not be overlooked that fluency constitutes just the initial stage of the creative process. Fluency has to be strongly coupled with, first, the selectivity to choose the more fundamental aspects of the problem to attend to, and second, the ability to identify which of the many alternatives are the best for solving the problem. Easy rhetoric, ebullient fantasy and mental dazzle that are unguided by these two factors do not guarantee adeptness in creative problem solving.

Exercise:

Test your fluency by naming at least *twelve* different possible uses for sunglasses.

Examples: Protect eyes from sunlight glare. Hide a black eye. Change appearance. Use for cutting. Hide hearing aid. Look like a movie star. Use as a mirror. Place on head to hold hair down. Protect eyes from dust, smog. Relieve headache caused by glare. Paperweight. Chew on ends during meetings, etc.

> *The realization that there are other points of view is the beginning of wisdom.*
> CHARLES M. CAMPBELL

Flexibility

The creative person is flexible in his thinking. He is able to choose and explore a wide variety of approaches to his problem without losing sight of his overall goal or purpose. During problem solving, if new developments or changed circumstances demand it, he can easily drop one line of thought, or an unworkable approach, and take up another. He shows resourcefulness in his ability to shift gears, to discard one frame of reference for another, to change perspective, stray off the beaten path, modify approaches and adapt quickly to new developments or requirements. He constantly asks himself, "What else?" or "What would happen if I viewed the problem from a different angle?"

Scientist James H. Austin distinguishes between two kinds of flexibility: "One is the tendency to shift from one category of meaning to another; the second is loose and unstructured meandering of attention, a readiness to free associate, to daydream, to unleash one's thoughts into broad unclassified paths only tangentially related either to the starting point or to each other." Austin feels that this second kind of flexibility correlates with the rapid production of original ideas.

The associative links between the idea components the creative person forms during problem solving are loose, fluid and capable of being dissociated and then reassembled into new patterns. He has no obsessional need to arrive at a closure by prematurely categorizing and structuring any of the elements he comes up with. He rather prefers to consider, test and weigh many configurations before deciding on one to solve his problem. Able to perceive a problem from different viewpoints, he can "bombard" it with a variety of possible solutions. He is free from what is termed the "hardening of the categories."

"Hardening of the categories" is frequently established as a result of overfamiliarity with certain objects. As the late professor John E. Arnold of Stanford University put it: "We see a pencil as only a writing instrument, we never see it as a tool for propping open a window, or as fuel for a fire, or as a means of defending ourselves in an attack. A pencil is a pencil. It is not a combination of graphite, wood, brass and rubber, each of which have multiple properties and multiple uses."

One area where many people lack flexibility is in asking questions. Not only is their repertoire of query limited, but they also lack the requisite situational flexibility to question in a way that would elicit other people's cooperation and support. Instead, their interrogative mode frequently tends to evoke a negative response.

Exercise:

Imagine that you're a manager of a department, with many subordinates reporting to you. Give several examples of: (1) effective questions that invite positive actions or response; (2) ineffective questions that turn other people off.

Examples of Effective Questions:
Open or direct questions employ the useful standbys who, what, when, where and how. They invite the subordinate to express openly what he or she feels or thinks. Examples: "How do you think we ought to handle this problem?" "What was your approach in solving this problem?" "Tell me, how do these new directives look to you?" "When will you be ready for the meeting with the committee?" "Do you have any ideas on how we can complete this project with three of our employees on sick leave?" These questions are usually to the point and invite the subordinate's cooperation. Implied in these questions is respect for the person's ability to solve problems.

Leading questions give a nonrestrictive direction to the reply. Examples: "How did you finally overcome the hitch to the problem?" "How did you go about correcting Mary's habitual tardiness?"

The planned or planted answer question invites the subordinate to give his or her opinion, even though there is an implied direction along the lines the manager thinks the problem could be effectively tackled. Implied also is the willingness to receive criticism or contradictory ideas. Examples: "How about using this approach?" "Would this procedure make sense to you?" "What would your ideas be on this . . . does it check with your experience?" "I love the idea that————, but can we add to that by ————?"

Unemotional questions appeal to reason and evoke little or no feeling. Examples: "What would be your first steps toward solving this problem?" "Any other thoughts about this problem?" "How can we use this idea to best advantage?"

Invitation to participate question lets the subordinate know that he or she can make a real contribution by expressing a view. Examples: "You could be of real help in this. What are your suggestions?" "How about this approach?" "What is your feeling about this?" "What do you think would be particularly useful about trying it this way?" "Can we improve on this?"

The off-the-hook question allows the subordinate to decline a request without losing face. Examples: "We have a serious overrun on this project. I don't suppose you would want to put in two or three extra hours tonight and tomorrow night?" "I can't afford the time to attend this convention. Could you possibly substitute for me?"

Invitation to comply question entails an order with the sting taken out of it by the tag line "OK?" or "right?" Example: "I know it is a lot of work, but we have to get it out by this evening. OK?"

Invitation to feedback question enables the manager to check on the subordinate's understanding of a task. Example: "Is it understood that after you've completed your survey of the department you'll check back with me with a complete report of your findings?"

Opening the feelings question invites the subordinate to reveal his or her true feelings. Examples: "I understand you didn't go along with the decision we reached at this morning's meeting. What is your concern about this—what is bothering you?" "What specifically is implied there that you don't like? What concerns you about it?"

Bringing out bashful ideas question asks for elaboration. Examples: "I am not sure I understand you correctly. Can you tell me more about what you have in mind?" "How might we do that?"

Examples of Ineffective Questions:

The squelcher question forces the subordinate to adopt a point of view with which he or she does not agree, or which forces the person to conform to a preconceived pattern. Examples: "Now if you were convinced that this approach is unfeasible, you wouldn't go along with it, would you?" "None of your ideas have worked out. What makes you think you could come up with a workable solution?" These questions usually reduce the subordinate's feeling of confidence in his or her creative competence and they may undermine the individual's initiative.

Dead-end questions drive the subordinate into a corner no matter what his or her answer may be. Example: "What made you think that the course of action you took was the only right one?"

Emotionally heated questions evoke negative feelings in the subordinate. Examples: "We've already tried this several times, so why do you insist on coming back with something that obviously won't work?" "I think you've talked long enough. Could you state your point briefly so we could make sense out of what you're saying?"

Impulse questions that just happen to occur to the manager. Example: "By the way, what do you think about the way Jane interrupted you at this morning's meeting?"

Trick questions that appear to ask for a frank opinion, but actually leave little choice for the subordinate to come up with a different solution. Example: "What should we do about Ann? Fire her or just transfer her out of your department?"

Mirror questions that simply invite compliance. Example: "Here's the way I'm going to accomplish this. Do you agree?"

Kill the idea questions that limit any consideration of developing the idea further. Example: "That is an excellent idea but it won't work in practice because————. I think we should try this approach instead. Don't you agree?"

There are two key don'ts to enhance mutual understanding and communication:

Don't settle for the answer to the primary question you ask, regardless of the response. Try to come back with a secondary question like: "Why is that?" "How do you happen to feel that way about it?"

Don't terminate communication by agreeing or disagreeing flatly with the response given. Keep the door open with noncommittal reinforcements like: "Umhum." "I see." "Oh, yes." "I see what you mean." Or simply repeat the message almost exactly as it was given. If the subordinate says, for example, "I believe we should give more authority to our employees," you might say, "You believe we should give more authority to our employees."

Still another way to keep the door wide open is simply to say nothing—and keep on saying nothing until the other person says what is on his or her mind. It is often not only the "pause that refreshes" but also an invitation to the other person to speak.

> *Sensitivity refers to a state of being aware of things as they really are rather than according to some predetermined set.*
> RALPH J. HALLMAN

Sensitivity to Problems

Philosopher John Dewey was one of the first to note that creativity does not start with facts, theories or hypotheses, but with a problematic situation. He felt that the ability to envisage and formulate the right problem, and to ask the right questions, is the crux of effective problem solving.

The creative person has keen powers of observation and an unusual ability to perceive and point out problems, situations and challenges that have escaped the attention of others. This is because of his (or her) greater sensitivity to the unusual or the promising aspects of the situations—the hidden opportunities often not perceived by other individuals. Hence he tends to be dissatisfied with things as they are and is eager to improve upon them. He is like the proverbial Socratic philosopher with a "thorn in his flesh," in that he is perpetually disturbed by something. For him there is hardly a situation entirely free of problems, but this does not cause him frustration and worry. On the contrary, he welcomes the challenge of problems and the state of "happy" dissatisfaction with the status quo. He knows that there are many as yet unlived possibilities of life and that creativity grows, as the poet A. E. Houseman speculated, out of irritation, like a pearl secreted from the friction-generating particle of sand in the oyster's shell.

Exercise:

In spite of equal opportunity legislation, women are still adversely affected by various stereotypes, superstitions and shibboleths when applying for a job they want.

List as many prevalent prejudices and biases as you can that discriminate against women in hiring situations.

Examples:

WOMEN

    change jobs too often.
    want to socialize too much.
    are not really interested in a career.
    don't take criticism well.
    will follow their spouses' job changes.

don't know what they really want.
don't like to work for women bosses.
don't like to work for men bosses.
waste too much time on gossip.
are too emotional.
are not achievement oriented.
are angry and bitter about their sex.
are not listened to by men bosses.
panic in crisis situations.

Now it's your turn. List at least *twenty* stereotypes.

Exercise:

The plight of older, unemployed persons in the job market is also due to a number of stereotypes and unfounded concepts.
List all the stereotypes you can think of that employers use to justify their reluctance to hire older people.

Examples:

OLDER PEOPLE

lack flexibility.
cannot concentrate.
tire easily.
are too slow.
resist change.
are overly sensitive to criticism.
are hostile toward new ideas.
are suspicious of co-workers.
cannot listen to others' complaints without getting irri–
tated.
are critical of their colleagues.
have poor attitudes toward work.
have no creativity left in them.

lack motivation.
have short attention spans.

Now list at least *twenty* other stereotypes.

The more we observe and are aware of,
the more mental connections we can make
that will result in new and relevant ideas.

MELISSA STRICKLAND

Originality

The creative person displays originality in his thinking. Since his thought processes are not jammed up with stereotypes he can reach out beyond the ordinary or commonplace, and think of more unusual, more unique solutions to his problems. His originality expresses itself also in his ability to take apart firmly structured and established systems, to dissolve existing syntheses and to use elements and concepts beyond the limits they possess in their primary contexts, to create a new combination, a new system of relationships.

Added to this ability to fragment and differentiate, the creative person is able to find unity in diversity, to see unexpected relationships and kinships, similarities, likenesses and connections between things, experiences and phenomena that to the noncreative person evidence no relationship whatever, until it is pointed out.

Because the creative person is always in quest of the new, he is usually generous toward unusual ideas, whether they be his own or others'. In fact, it has been noted that the creative person's open-mindedness sometimes extends to the point of gullibility in accepting bizarre or even crackpot ideas, and that this agile and playful imagination toys around with such notions quite seriously before relegating them to the dustbin. New perspectives, new ideas and venturesome conceptions provide an endless source of exercise for his mind.

Originality feeds on change. It is for this reason that many creative individuals—through travel and immersion in new happenings—perpetually seek to reexperience, time and again, the quality of freshness and the feeling of novelty.

Exercise:

Give original interpretations and definitions for these phrases and terms often used in business organizations.

1. A program
2. Channels
3. Coordinator
4. Consultant (or expert)
5. To activate
6. To implement a program
7. Under consideration
8. Under active consideration
9. A meeting
10. A conference
11. Reliable source
12. Informed source
13. Unimpeachable source
14. A clarification
15. We're making a survey
16. To note and initial
17. "See me"
18. Let's get together on this
19. We will advise you in due course
20. To give someone the picture

Examples:

1. A program—Any assignment that cannot be completed by one phone call.
2. Channels—The trail left by interoffice memos.
3. Coordinator—The guy who has the desk between two expediters.

4. Consultant (or expert)—Any ordinary guy more than 50 miles from home.
5. To activate—To make carbons and add more names to the memo.
6. To implement a program—Add more names to the memo.
7. Under consideration—Never heard of it.
8. Under active consideration—We're looking for it in the files.
9. A meeting—A mass nulling by masterminds.
10. A conference—A place where conversation is substituted for the dreariness of labor.
11. Reliable source—The guy you just met.
12. Informed source—The guy who told the guy you met.
13. Unimpeachable source—The guy who started the rumor to begin with.
14. A clarification—To fill in the background with so many details that the foreground goes underground.
15. We're making a survey—We need more time to think of an answer.
16. To note and initial—Let's spread around the responsibility for this.
17. "See me"—Come down to my office, I'm lonesome and need help.
18. Let's get together on this—I'm assuming you are as confused as I am.
19. We will advise you in due course—If we figure it out, we will let you know.
20. To give someone the picture—A long, confused and inaccurate statement to a newcomer.

When you stop learning, stop listening,
stop looking and asking questions, always
new questions, then it is time to die.
LILLIAN SMITH

Curiosity

Creativity is contingent upon the preservation of the curiosity and sense of wonder that is so apparent in youth, and so conspicuously absent in many grownups. The educational and developmental processes most people go through, while ostensibly preparing them for the responsibilities of adulthood, nevertheless manage to conventionalize them to a point where lively curiosity and wonder almost cease to exist. In addition, or perhaps as a consequence of this, many adults have a deep distrust of curiosity, imagination and fantasy making. They often show this by their trigger-ready tendency to criticize or dismiss thoughts that cannot be defended by facts or logic. There is little doubt that this closed-mindedness has conditioned much of our social environment with a timid cautiousness, preventing many valuable ideas from taking root.

Children have a keen and intense awareness of their environment. They have a ready feeling of curiosity toward everything they touch or experience. They have a precious propulsion toward seeking understanding, toward piercing the mystery they sense in everything they perceive.

The rapt sense of children's wonder and their avid interest in the minutest details of their surroundings disappears sooner than all the other characteristics of childhood. Only the truly creative individual manages to retain his pristine sense of curiosity. And it is this lively attitude of curiosity and inquiry that enables the creative person to constantly enrich and add to the store of information and experience that he draws upon when creatively engaged.

Another noteworthy characteristic of the creative person's wide-awake interest and attitude of inquiry is that it invariably extends far beyond the confines of his specialization or main line of work. His wide spectrum of interest embraces many related and unrelated areas and fields, and he can get excited about almost any problem or phenomenon that puzzles or mystifies him. Many things that are taken for granted by others are for him pregnant with mystery, puzzlement and challenge. In this sense he is intellectually restless, not satisfied with what is accepted, established, or known, constantly wondering how things could or might be, always ready to consider and visualize new possibilities. He feels that it is necessary to improve upon, or add to, existing concepts. It is said that necessity is the mother of invention, but there has been a curious lack of interest in discovering the father. Could it be that the father is curiosity?

Exercise:

Let's assume you have been invited to be a host or hostess of a TV talk show that includes a panel of "experts" on the topic you've chosen. In order to satisfy not only your curiosity, but that of millions of potential viewers, you have to formulate questions that are evocative and that probe the unproven assumptions and questionable statements made about the topic. Pick a topic, and as a first order of business, write down all the questionable or faulty ideas and assumptions that have been made on the topic.

Examples:
Although the female liberationists' crusade to correct various inequalities in our society has been valuable and commendable, a great many pronouncements and ideas are not only counterproductive, but downright harmful to the cause. A list of a few arguments that could be posed to a panel of liberationist leaders would include the following:

- Men repress women and force them to be what they are.
- Marriage was created by males for the exploitation of female labor.
- Women are not paid fairly for their work.
- It is degrading to do housework.
- Men refuse to talk to women about anything important.
- Women must live vicariously through men.

Now it's your turn.

The awful thing is that you can never be aware of what you are not aware of.
EDWARD DE BONO

Openness to Feelings and the Unconscious

The creative person has more energy, is more impulsive, and is more responsive to emotions and feelings than the less creative person. Since he is more in touch with, and open to, his feelings he has a better access to the buried materials in his unconscious. Or, to put it differently, because of his relative lack of defensive distortions, inhibitions and repressions he is able to have a more direct and uncluttered pipeline to the real world of ideas in the unconscious.

According to psychologist Abraham H. Maslow, the really creative person is one who accepts his essentially *androgynous* character:

> This is the person who can live with his unconscious; live with, let's say, his childishness, his fantasy, his imagination, his wish fulfillment, his femininity, his poetic quality, his crazy quality. He is the person, as one psychoanalyst said in a nice phrase, "who can regress in the service of the ego." This is voluntary regression. This person is the one who has that kind of creativeness at his disposal, readily available, that I think we're interested in.

According to Maslow's theory, there are two distinct kinds of creativity: primary creativity and secondary creativity. Primary creativity is of the kind that: emerges from the unconscious; is the source of new discovery, novelty and ideas that depart from what exists at the moment; is common and universal to all people; is found in healthy children; exists in those who are able to play, dream, laugh and loaf, those who can be spontaneous, more open to unconscious promptings and impulses; is present in those who accept their softness, femininity and some weakness; is found more among individuals who have a keen interest in the artistic and aesthetic fields.

On the other hand, secondary creativity is of the kind that: comes from the conscious, primarily; exists in rigid, constricted people who are afraid of their unconscious and who are cautious and careful in everything they do, in those who can't play very well and who excessively control their emotions; is characteristic of those individuals who demand a high degree of order in their lives and who dislike poetry and other emotional expression; is present among those who drown their childishness and who are afraid of their softness, femininity, and who repress all weakness.

According to Maslow, the healthy creative person is not one who uses exclusively the primary or the secondary processes, but one who has managed a fusion, or synthesis, of both the primary and the secondary processes, of the conscious and the unconscious, of the deeper self and the conscious self.

Since the creative person puts greater trust in feelings and intuitive sensings, he (or she) is readily able to utilize them as guides to steer him toward unique solutions of his problems. When judging the relevance of ideas that come to him during the creative process, he measures their appropriateness or belongingness by their feeling of fit and harmony.

Exercise:

One of the most useful tools to elicit and make you aware of your true and spontaneous attitudes, feelings and emotions is the incomplete sentence. Whereas a direct question about a "private" subject, such as feelings and emotions, often produces a censored and distorted response—even in the privacy of an individual's own mind—the incomplete sentence elicits a true, unadorned reaction.

Write out your responses to the following incomplete sentences. This will enable you to get in touch with your real feelings.

Examples:

When people disagree with me———I disagree with them to get even.

When people disagree with me———I think they must be right.

When people disagree with me———I think they're stupid.

Now complete these sentences:

1. When I make a mistake, I———.
2. The most valuable things in my life———.
3. When I'm criticized I———.
4. I would most like to be———.
5. When I'm emotionally upset I———.
6. My future seems———.
7. When I'm not understood, I———.
8. Happiness is determined mainly———.
9. I avoid———.
10. Things would be better if———.
11. I'm appalled at———.
12. I often enjoy———.
13. I feel guilty when———.
14. I feel warmest toward———.
15. I lack———.
16. Life is good———.
17. When I run into bad situations, I———.
18. I'm incapable of———.
19. I get annoyed with people who———.
20. The subjects that are too touchy to speak of are———.
21. If I'm not accepted or listened to at a party I———.
22. Self-respect comes from———.
23. I am moody when———.
24. I look forward to———.

25. I become angry at others————.
26. I get real pleasure————.
27. When people interrupt me I————.
28. Praise and compliments————.
29. What I want most in life is————.
30. My best days are————.

Motivation

Basic to creative achievement is a strong desire to create. The creative person derives great satisfaction from his creative activities and is keenly interested in his chosen work. Any difficulties that he inevitably encounters do not discourage him. He welcomes problems as personal challenges and looks forward to the time when he can grapple with them. He assumes an optimistic stance vis-à-vis his problems and feels, like Pogo, that he is "confronted with insurmountable opportunities."

The creative person likes to pursue problems that are intrinsically of high interest and is governed and guided more by inner stimulus than by outer demand. He (or she) creates not because someone wants him to create, but because he must.

The highly creative individual is frequently haunted by his problems and he cannot let go of them. Anyone who has observed the creative person at work has been impressed by the fully absorbed and vigorous concentration that infuses his activity. His strong sense of purpose and commitment and the intensity in his encounter with problems show strong ego-involvement. And this ego-involvement is responsible for the unusual staying power the creative individual exhibits.

The creative person is ready to engage in meaningful problem solving purely for the satisfaction that it provides, even when no other reward lies ahead. This explains why he (or she) goes to great lengths to find problems that are most inclusive of his interests and a real challenge to all of his capacities. His motives are more internal and goal centered than competitive, and he is not unduly influenced by what others may be expecting of him.

His chosen work is the most important avenue for the fulfillment of his life and his striving for completion. He is fully dedicated to what he is doing and this provides him with a sense of joy. Unlike many people, he is not preoccupied with the pursuit of happiness, but finds rather his happiness in the pursuit of his creative activities.

Exercises:

Frequently we feel unmotivated because we are unclear about our key needs and the working environment that would bring out our best efforts.

The following two exercises are designed to clarify your needs and values, and what you would expect from an *ideal* working environment.

1. Rate Your Key Needs

Indicate your first, second, third, fourth and fifth most important choices by 1, 2, 3, 4 and 5.

_____Economic security
_____Stimulating environment
_____Recognition by superiors
_____Respect from subordinates
_____Recognition by the general public
_____Recognition by friends
_____Pleasant location
_____Variety in the job
_____Learning opportunities and growth

_____Use of abilities
_____Independence, freedom
_____Opportunity to be creative
_____Time for self or family
_____Achievement
_____Contribute to society
_____Power over people
_____Influence over policy
_____Self-determination
_____Money
_____Travel
_____Other_____
_____Other_____
_____Other_____
_____Other_____

2. Ideal Working Environment

Complete these sentences by filling in the line with a statement that seems appropriate to your idea of an ideal working environment. Work quickly and give your *first* impression. Try to make each statement a single idea that is *crucial* to your needs.

In my ideal job environment, I want:

1. A boss who_____.
2. The attitude of my co-workers to be _____.
3. A company that_____.
4. To use skills that_____.
5. To get recognition for_____.
6. A location that_____.
7. Freedom to_____.
8. The pay to be_____.
9. Working hours to be_____.
10. To travel_____.
11. To advance_____.
12. Important changes_____.

13. My abilities _____.
14. Differences of opinion between _____:
15. The decisions _____.
16. Information _____.
17. Working conditions _____.
18. ??? _____.

Now review the statements you made and then make the decisions that follow:

Write the numbers of the six most important statements.
_____ _____ _____ _____ _____ _____

From the six statements, choose the four most important.
_____ _____ _____ _____

From the four statements, choose the two most important.
_____ _____

From the two statements, choose the one most important. _____

This decision making process is very important in helping you identify your priorities when you are faced with new career choices, or in changing the career you now have.

> *Success depends upon staying power. The reason for failure in most cases is lack of perseverance.*
> JAMES RUSSELL MILLER

Persistence and Concentration

An enormous capacity for taking pains, a dogged persistence in the face of difficulties and frustrations and a vast amount of sheer arduous work are some of the additional outstanding attributes of creative persons. These qualities stand out in their biographies, and are also the ones emphasized most when they counsel others with creative aspirations.

The popular notion that the creative individual relies mainly on effortless inspiration and unforced spontaneity is still a widespread misconception. It is not fully realized that creative achievement requires confidence, the maintenance of morale, and long-lasting pervasive excitement to stubbornly resist premature discouragement in the face of difficulties and temporary failures. Although the creative person occasionally experiences failure, he is not downed, crushed or maimed by it. He feels that any bad luck he experiences is only temporary and will exhaust itself if he continues to persist.

From talking to highly creative individuals, it becomes clear that the majority of them do not know what a mere forty-hour work week means. Their preoccupation with problems is incessant. Occasionally they may have moments in their work that are crowned with joy; frequently, however, the intense struggle with problems does not yield immediate solutions.

As Einstein once remarked, "I think and think, for months, for years. Ninety-nine times the conclusion is false. The hundredth time I am right."

Creation is preceded by hard thinking, prolonged reflection and concentrated hard work. There is a continuous assimilation of new knowledge and experience, a steady pondering on the causes of the difficulties that are met with regularly, and a sorting out of hunches and ideas that flash across the firmament of consciousness. It's apparent that all this takes time and a willingness to experience and accept many agonies along the route. Occasionally, these conscious efforts may even appear excessive. It is almost proverbial how many creative individuals have threatened—especially when their wastepaper baskets overflow with discarded work sheets—to quit their work for good. But the next day they are back, probing and attacking problems, determined to complete what is unfinished.

Quite often in the beginning stages of creative problem

solving the conscious efforts are abortive and useless; and creative individuals have testified how many times they had to, temporarily, give up their efforts, how many initial attempts ended in failure, before a valid solution or idea emerged. Still, all these apparently futile initial efforts are not as wasted as they seem; they serve the function of activating the unconscious processes of cerebration and incubation. Without preparatory work, the unconscious can be notoriously unproductive.

It is true that some creative persons rely more deliberately on the gestative process of the unconscious to complete ideas for them. With most creators, however, a dogged and intense preliminary effort constitutes the necessary prelude to original production. The capacity for original work grows out of long training, constant application and unflagging persistence.

Since, in the course of creative work, a lessening of persistence frequently occurs—sometimes due to repeated failures, at other times to lessening of interest—it serves well to learn to cope with this reaction.

Discomfort with persistence or a feeling of flagging interest is often a signal for the need to get away from a problem and to relax for a while. Creative individuals often find that they can relax by working on another challenging problem. Many of them say that they function best when involved in several undertakings simultaneously, each at a different stage of development, each affording an opportunity to relax when necessary.

The creative process also requires concentration and continuous thinking to a degree where the creative person becomes oblivious to his surroundings. During the creative process he maintains an uninterrupted rapport with his unconscious and formulates the emerging proposals into something that makes sense. This requires disciplined concentration. Philosopher Richard Guggenheimer explains it this way:

A great disciplinary effort is required for most productive minds before they reach a stage where they are able to swiftly launch themselves into completely spontaneous absorption in the creative business at hand. A thousand and one diverting thoughts must be suppressed; the mind must brush aside myriad temptations to amble here and there along the enticing byways of casual thinking. It must become totally involved in the mounting wave of its deep intent. The principal labor is getting the wave started; most of us splash about in our thinking and mistake the ripples of our noisy commotion for real movement.

Of course, when there is a complete and wholehearted absorption in the business at hand, the activity itself helps the process along. Suggestions on how to proceed occur spontaneously. The creative person no longer has to use his energy to force his mind to concentrate on the problem. Where great disciplinary effort is invariably required, however, is at the beginning stages of the problem solving process. It is at these stages that many extraneous thoughts must be discarded or suppressed in order to plug into the creative current.

Exercises:

1. Here is an exercise to tax and increase your persistence and powers of concentration. While it looks deceptively easy, it is in reality quite difficult to write a composition in which each succeeding word begins with the next letter of the alphabet.

Write a composition or a story in which the first word begins with *A* and the last with *Z*. And all the words in between have as their first letter the letters of the alphabet sequentially from *A* to *Z*.

There are no requirements as to a specific subject matter.

Examples:
"Another beautiful, cool day, excellent for going hiking," I jested, knowing lazy Mary Norton ordinarily preferred quiet relaxation. She teased, "Utterly vacuous, wild, Xavier. You're zany!"

A beautiful child's demeaning expression frightened Gustav Humbert. "I just keep lascivious mentations nonapparent, or perhaps, quietly repress sexy thoughts. Ubiquitously, variously, women x your zeal."

2. A creative individual is capable of intense concentration. But rather than only being able to concentrate on what interests him, the creative person is also able to concentrate on those things that are *necessary* for his work. To develop concentration, visualization is one of the direct paths.

With your eyes closed, in your mind's eye, draw a white chalk circle on a blackboard. Imagine the blackboard. Imagine the circle. Imagine a white chalk dot in the center of the circle. Imagine the dot and circle in front of your eyes approximately one foot away. Practice until you can hold it for one minute, then two, then three minutes.

If at first you find it difficult, *write* out the instructions in the above paragraph to "prime" your mental pump. Copy the paragraph as many times as necessary until you can do it without first copying the paragraph. When you can hold the image for three minutes, with your eyes closed, begin the same exercise with your eyes open, and continue to practice until you can visualize the image for three minutes, with your eyes open.

> *I find that images appear only if we give our ideas uncontrolled freedom—when we are dreaming while awake. As soon as full consciousness, voluntary consciousness, returns, images weaken, darken; they seem to withdraw to some unknown region.*
> ALFRED BINET

Ability to Think in Images

Creative people rely heavily on internal visual imagery or "thought-visions." These are, at times, exceptionally clear and complete; at other times they can be murky and tied loosely to an assortment of vague and meandering thoughts. But whether clear or murky, imagery frequently contains the kernel of a new, original idea.

It was an image analogy that started atomic physics. To find an explanation for the atomic structure of elements, Niels Bohr used the image of tiny spheres circling in orbits, and to get some insight into the processes within the atom, he made use of the image picture of a miniature planetary system. Einstein likewise claimed that he rarely thought in words at all. Notions came to him in images and only later did he try to express these in words. And there are a whole host of other noted creative individuals on record who stated that they first try to *feel* or couch in *imagery* what they imagine, before naming or formulating a verbal concept of it.

Language, of course, can and does exert a tremendous influence on both the unconscious direction of thinking and on how the thoughts are finally formed and articulated. But this influence can often be harmful. This is because of the readiness of language to name, to label, to form concepts on what is perceived internally. This frequently limits any further development of the incipient ideas.

Most people are impatient with the vagueness and incoherence of ideas during the beginning stages of the creative process. They feel immediately compelled to force them into the familiar mold of already existing frameworks, or into language and concepts that invariably fail to do justice to the singular qualities of the perceived novelty. The attempt to crystallize the initially dim or vague creative concept forces a premature closure on the idea which prevents the full range of novelty from finding expression.

The precision forced on images and complex thoughts through premature articulation is also fraught with the danger of actually altering them. The renowned mathematician Jacques Hadamaard states:

> I feel some uneasiness when I see that Locke and similarly John Stuart Mill considered the use of words necessary whenever complex ideas are implied. I think, on the contrary, and

so will a majority of creative people, that the more complicated and difficult a question is, the more we should distrust words, the more we should feel we must control that dangerous ally and its sometimes treacherous precision.

In this connection it might be of interest also to cite philosopher F. S. C. Northrop's ideas on the subject. He stated that,

> If one wants to get pure facts he must go not to physicists or to chemists or to engineers, but to impressionistic painters. They give us the pure qualities, just the impressions, not the objects we infer from them. . . . The person in our society today who shows us what is directly observed is the impressionistic painter. He just paints this field of immediacy with the sensuous qualities and says, "Now just stop with those and enjoy them." I believe that one of the greatest sources of creativity is to be found in being pulled back by the modern, Western, impressionistic painters to that which is sensed immediately. Only thus are we broken loose from our older inferred theories and enabled to start over again.

What Northrop means is that one should sense what one perceives before articulating it, before making it conceptual or symbolic, or simply before trying to *understand* it intellectually. In this essentially feeling-sensorial fashion we can make our perceptions more original and creative. And if we can incorporate observations creatively, then we can also immeasurably increase our capacity to think creatively.

Exercise:

Remember the famous fable of the five blind men and the elephant? As the story goes, five blind men were trying to describe what an elephant looked like by touching the animal at various points on its body. The first blind man, feeling the elephant's thick and enormous leg, announced that the elephant was rather like a large tree stump. The second blind man, with his hands on the elephant's tail, disagreed, saying the elephant was more like a whip. The third blind man, having felt the elephant's ears, said they were both wrong, that the elephant was shaped like a large lily pad. The fourth blind man, seated upon the elephant's back, said, "No, you're all wrong, the elephant is shaped like a tortoise shell." This announcement didn't sit well at all with the fifth blind man, who had just finished feeling the elephant's trunk, and who thought the elephant to be more like a thick snake.

Now imagine the five blind men touching at various points a cow, a giraffe, a horse, or any animal of your own choosing. What possible images could they form in their minds just through touch?

> *I suspect that almost all creativity is really the result of play, in the higher meaning of the word.*
> SIDNEY J. PARNES

Ability to Toy with Ideas

There is, frequently, a seemingly light side to the creative person's involvement in his work. It is shown in his tendency to become lost in what to an outsider seems like an irresponsible playing with ideas, forms, materials, relationships, concepts and elements which he shapes into all kinds of incongruous and imaginative combinations. The creative person knows from experience that this apparently purposeless testing and toying with possibilities strengthens, at the same time that it loosens, his imaginative powers. It is a "letting go" exercise out of which significant creative ideas often emerge.

This toying and improvising also serves some very concrete and immediate purpose. It often helps creative individuals to "chance upon" creative solutions to recalcitrant problems—problems that had previously defied any direct frontal attack. But most importantly, playful improvising and the willingness to view a problem from unusual angles helps them to capture a mood that facilitates the flow of ideas. Then, one idea that occurs will pull out another and this in turn another, until one idea is hit upon that suddenly commands their full attention because they feel that this idea represents something truly novel.

Creative individuals have also learned from past experience that these quasi-serious exercises relax the critical and conservative bent of their consciousness. A lighthearted spirit of play frees them from the habits, conditionings and conventions that impede the arrival of the novel. By putting the judicial censor of their conscious minds to sleep, so to speak, they can pass over the established order and set the stage for the premiere of novel ideas and solutions.

Exercise:

Since it is better to laugh at life rather than lament over it—especially in these enervating eighties that just began—write at least *five* original epigrammatical thoughts that in some way reflect on contemporary living. Be as whimsical, humorous or playful as you can.

Examples:
1. If life hands you a lemon, squeeze it and start a lemonade stand.

    —Unknown
2. It is not true that life is one damn thing after another—it's one damn thing over and over.

    —EDNA ST. VINCENT MILLAY
3. Life is one long process of getting tired.

    —SAMUEL BUTLER
4. Don't lose faith in humanity: think of all the people in the United States who have never played you a single nasty trick.

    —ELBERT HUBBARD

5. If you see good in everybody, you may be an optimist. And then again you may be nuts.

—BREWSTER BLADE

6. In the journey through life, many cross the wrong bridges, others burn the right ones, and the rest try to make it in a leaky boat.

—EUGENE RAUDSEPP

7. For that tired, run-down feeling, try jaywalking.

—FARMER'S ALMANAC

8. If you can keep your head when all about you are losing theirs, perhaps you don't understand the situation.

—MIKE CONNOLLY

9. Today, if you are not confused you are just not thinking clearly.

—IRENE PETER

10. Life is easier to take than you'd think; all that is necessary is to accept the impossible, do without the indispensable and bear the intolerable.

—KATHLEEN HARRIS

*It is axiomatic that to think intelligently
is to think creatively.*
ALEX F. OSBORN

Ability to Analyze and Synthesize

The creative person is able to analyze and break down a problem into parts and to perceive the relationships that exist between the parts and the whole. Analysis is frequently thought of as being diametrically opposed to creativity, but it is part and parcel of the ability to synthesize. Prolonged searching and analysis almost always precede creative synthesis; they are complementary aspects of a single process in creative problem solving.

Analysis is necessary because it helps the creative person to break the problem down into manageable elements. Synthesizing creatively means combining or rearranging many elements in a way that results in the formation of a new whole. Thus, the creative person has strong dual abilities, both to abstract the details and to synthesize or orchestrate a new configuration.

That creative people tend to spend more time in the analytical phases of problem solving than less creative individuals has been documented by several experiments. For example, psychologist Gary A. Steiner states:

> Experiments have indicated that highly creative individuals often spend more time in the initial stages of problem formulation, in broad scanning of alternatives. Less creative individuals are more apt to "get on with it." For example, in problems divisible into analytic and synthetic stages, highs spend more time on the former—in absolute as well as relative terms. As a result, they may leapfrog lows in the later stages of the solutions process. Having disposed of more blind alleys, they are able to make more comprehensive integrations.

Researchers S. I. Blatt and M. I. Stein reached a similar conclusion with their experiments:

> Our more creative individuals spent more time and asked more questions that were oriented to analyzing the problem. Our less creative individuals, on the other hand, spent more time and asked more questions that were oriented to synthesizing the information they had. Our observations suggest that the more creative men were "feeling out" the problem, attempting to understand it, to become one with it; and, after they understood what they were about, they then integrated what they had learned. Consequently, they spent more time analyzing the problem and less time synthesizing the information they had. Our less creative individuals looked as if they were going to wrench the solution from the problem, to dominate it; they "went after" the answer even before they knew the structure of the problem.

Exercise:

To increase your ability to analyze and to synthesize, formulate a series of pairs of attributes that in your mind would characterize an *ideal* leader of people. Each pair of formulations should synthesize what are usually considered polar opposites.

Examples:
1. Good sense of realism combined with imagination.
2. Ability to identify with subordinates, while retaining a certain psychological distance.
3. Courage to say no, but willing to compromise if need be.
4. Ability to inspire, while keeping subordinates under control.
5. Ability to find faults, without losing sight of main issues.
6. Ability to take care of immediate problems, without losing sight of future problems.
7. Ability to consider problems as they pertain to a particular department, while considering their importance to the company as a whole.
8. Openness to suggestions of others, but capable of making autonomous decisions.
9. Ability to make quick decisions, but also able to defer decision making until the problem has matured.
10. Ability to delegate authority, while keeping control of those things that happen within his field of responsibility.
11. Growth-minded, yet able to retain what has been consolidated in the past.
12. Drive to attain measurable results quickly, but able to handle long-range, slow-moving projects and operations.

Now it's your turn. Aim for at least *ten* such descriptions.

*The better the idea, the more likely it is
to have been extremely vague.*
D. O. HEBB

Tolerance of Ambiguity

One significant reason many people are lacking in ability
to produce creative ideas is their strong preference for precise
and concrete thoughts. As a consequence, they tend to prematurely reject notions and ideas that do not fit into what
they already know, or that are too intangible or elusive to
permit immediate comprehension and categorization. Any
vagueness is experienced as a scary, uncomfortable, and
sometimes even an irresponsible state of mind by many
people because of their predilection for clarity and effortless
understanding. The clearly defined and familiar have a powerful hold on most people because the new threatens to disturb the secure comfort of the familiar. As William J. J. Gordon explains this:

> All problems present themselves to the mind as threats of fail-
> ure. For someone striving to win in terms of a successful solu-
> tion, this threat evokes a mass response in which the most
> immediate superficial solution is clutched frantically as a
> balm to anxiety. . . . Yet if we are to perceive all the impli-
> cations and possibilities of the new we must risk at least tem-
> porary ambiguity and disorder. Human beings are heir to a
> legacy of frozen words and ways of perceiving that wrap their
> world in comfortable familiarity.

The hold of the familiar precludes the possibility of per-
mitting the unguided imaginative promptings that emerge
during the creative process to have spontaneous free play.

The truly creative person is not afraid of disorder or ambiguity. On the contrary, he (or she) seems rather attracted to
phenomena that are not fully ordered or readily compre-
hended, and prefers cognitively challenging and complex situations. As a result, he is aware of, and open to, the intricate,

confusing and paradoxical qualities of most situations. There is no fear-motivated desire to close out any conflicting or ambiguous elements he encounters. Like all human beings, he seeks integration and order, but he is willing to seek it without shutting out of his awareness the chaotic or the ambiguous.

In his work, the creative person is always ready to relax any binding habit patterns, and adheres as little as possible to preconceived plans or stereotyped approaches. He also shows his pliability by being able to simultaneously consider and weigh different or even conflicting concepts and frames of reference.

The creative person shows his greater plasticity and adaptability while creating, and he has a healthy respect for groping and uncertainty while forming and ordering his thoughts.

Exercise:

Either/or, or pro and con, situations are often ambiguous and controversial. To test and develop your ability to synchronously consider opposing frames of reference try this exercise:

One current controversy in business and industry concerns the problem of whether creativity should be encouraged in individuals or in groups. Give at least *five* arguments in favor of group creativity, and *five* arguments favoring individual creativity.

Examples:
Progroup:
   1. A group's creative effort in problem solving is synergistic in that the solution they arrive at is better and more effective than is the sum of individual contributions arrived at in solo efforts.
   2. Groups provide systematic opportunities for crossfertilization of ideas, which is imperative for best results.
   3. There is more stimulation and "spark" in group work.

4. Creativity is more predictable and better controlled in group effort. The forces of competition will not permit waiting for illumination or inspiration of the individualistic creative variety.
5. Groups do not have the fear of criticism that often exists in the loose, individualistic approach.
6. A creative person will be more productive when working in a group. The number of stimuli setting his brain in motion is multiplied.
7. Groups stimulate discussion, pooling of knowledge and exposure to different viewpoints.

Proindividual:
1. True creativity is an individual process.
2. A group can only build upon, combine or evaluate the ideas and concepts of individuals.
3. Groups do not create an idea. They can only operate to act, not to think. Groups do not intuitively or imaginatively see into the future; only a single person can do that.
4. Group function erects certain psychological barriers that impede creativity. It frightens bold and original thought.
5. The really creative people need to be alone and free to work solo. Team approach requires a passion for anonymity.
6. Most of the landmarks of creativity and invention have been established by only a few lone creators.
7. The oversystematized, overcontrolled and overcoordinated efforts of teams and groups put brakes on creative thinking by precluding broad outlook, imaginative journeys into areas other than those of immediate concern, and the quiet incubative state which is so essential for original, creative departures.
8. Collaborative work increases the suppression of individual initiative and courage. It is well known that teamwork suffers from the pull of the lowest common denominator—the most daring idea to come out of a

group represents the most daring idea of the least daring member.

Discernment and Selectivity

The overemphasis among the investigators of creativity on the factor of *fluency* may have overshadowed the importance of another attribute frequently overlooked entirely in the discussions about the creative process. This is the ability to discern the fundamentals in a problem. This factor of discernment, the sensing of relevance, the intuitive feelings of what is significant, is, in some ways, opposed to fluency, but is perhaps as crucial an attribute for creativity as the ability to generate a large number of ideas.

Creative persons differ from the less creative or the noncreative ones in the way they select elements to attend to when confronting a problem. They are better able to judge which factors must be taken into account and which can be neglected or discarded without risk of error. They are also able to discard irrelevant ideas, however original, that simply do not fit, whereas a merely fluent person can get his attention tangled up amid a jungle of possibilities. In addition, the creative individual shows his selectivity in his ability to organize his work as economically as the objectives allow. He or she won't allow any superfluous clutter to ruin the elegance of creative solutions.

In creative problem solving it is, as a rule, not necessarily the individual who is ebulliently fluent about a problem, nor the one who reaches the highest degree of abstraction in analysis, who shows the highest degree of creativity. Whether fluent or not, the individual who can grasp the heart of the matter frequently evidences the highest degree of creativity. In creative thinking it is the *quality* that counts and not necessarily the *quantity* of ideas produced. Quantity can add up to nothing if the central point is missed. Creativity is a matter of penetrating to the essence, of discerning the true crux of the problem, rather than merely exhibiting a wealth of notions and ideas.

The creative individual is guided by a hunch or an intuitive feeling that enables him (or her) to exercise choice, taste and discernment. It is the intuitive feeling that enables him to make valid distinctions in the complex interplay of elements with which he is dealing. Without this feeling he not only misses much of significance, but is apt to get lost in a welter of irrelevancies.

Exercise:

More valuable and expensive time is wasted in unproductive meetings than in almost any other communication function. Since the success of a meeting depends heavily on the quality of leadership it receives, test your discernment by pointing out the most important attributes and actions an effective discussion leader should exhibit.

Examples:
The leader
1. Must restrain his own desire for self-expression so the group may have adequate opportunity to discuss the scheduled problems. He needs, however, the ability to ask stimulating and exploring questions.
2. Must have a feeling of genuine fellowship with others, marked by his courteousness to and sincere interest in the group members.
3. Has to be fair-minded and open-minded, show a high degree of impartiality and tactfulness, and be receptive to suggestions and constructive criticism.

4. Is able to use humor at appropriate times to draw off negative feelings.
5. Must have the ability to inspire confidence in others and have the human relations skill to motivate the group members to explore the issues in depth.
6. Never sticks stubbornly to his point of view, but is willing to yield when necessary for the progress of the group.
7. Has to have the ability to see the obvious and not introduce complexity where a shortcut is possible.
8. Is able to mediate and reconcile differences of opinion.

Among the unpleasant features that the discussion leader may encounter are the various meeting misbehaviors by problem participants. Pinpoint some of the main undesirable meeting behaviors and what the discussion leader could do about them.

For example, one problem the discussion leader may encounter is that of whispered side conversation carried on during the session, especially when a large number of people participate. These conversations may, on occasion, become highly distracting and may split the group into several fragmentary and noncontributory cliques. One of the most effective ways of dealing with this problem is to interrupt the general discussion abruptly. Frequently a whispered remark is highly relevant to the discussion.

Also undesirable is the tendency of some participants to monopolize the entire group discussion. This behavior slows the pace of the meeting and tends to divide the group. Sometimes the verbose member is incapable of submitting his contribution in a few short, clear sentences, or he may be too eager to present several ideas at once.

A more serious case of monopolization is presented by the speaker who not only talks too long, but too often and on the wrong occasions. He usually also interrupts other speakers, confusing the discussion and annoying the persons interrupted.

As a rule, the monopolizer is also a bad listener; consequently there are many irrelevancies in his arguments. If the discussion leader is familiar with the argument presented, he should politely interrupt the speaker, either by asking a relevant question or by stating the point himself.

It takes courage to be creative, just as soon as you have a new idea, you're in the minority of one.
E. PAUL TORRANCE

Ability to Tolerate Isolation

When ready to work, the creative person isolates himself from the distractions and interruptions of his environment in order to establish a receptive, leisurely mood. He arranges circumstances so that he can be completely alone, undisturbed and solely concentrated on the creative task at hand.

In addition to his ability to comfortably tolerate extended periods of physical withdrawal from others, the creative person is also able to tolerate a measure of *psychological isolation*. If he works in an organization, this means that he attempts to purge his creative deliberations from such considerations as scheduling, costs, his superior's pet ideas about the approaches to the problem and most of the other prosaic demands of corporate life. Any extraneous considerations that get grafted onto his problem can block the emergence of novel ideas. They can act as barriers by inducing anxiety and guilt feelings because he is not doing what is expected or demanded of him. Ideally, he should be allowed to let his mind work at its own pace and in conformity to its own natural and congenial way. Although the creative person requires periods of privacy and is frequently considered to be a "lone wolf," he is seldom withdrawn, isolated or uncommunicative.

It should be pointed out, however, that excessively prolonged periods of isolation from others tend to deflate and devitalize rather than enhance the capacity to create. Imagination, when isolated or encapsulated, shrinks and shrivels. It has to be occasionally nourished by active immersion and participation with others. But the creative person cannot allow undue influence from others. He has to retain a safe margin of social distance in order to do justice to his creative potential.

Since the creative process is in actuality a private and internally motivated affair, the creative individual has to have the courage and ego strength to face a sense of inner loneliness when venturing into the unknown. Once he is committed to this no-return path it is well-nigh impossible for him to fall back on somebody else or to share the responsibility and the development of his idea. Although teamwork projects are very popular these days, the creative person seldom fulfills his potential capacities through collaboration. In the realm of genuine creativity there is only one solo instrument: the private individual mind and personality of the creator. As Carl R. Rogers has stated: "One cannot be creative without being out there and alone; the extent of the aloneness depends on the extent of the creativity. The more creative the act, the more completely alone one is." And the lone creator frequently needs all the courage and self-confidence he can muster to stand up to the criticisms leveled toward his idea, for any radically new idea almost always encounters a mountain of resistance and criticism.

The need for isolation and detachment does not mean that the creative individual can totally dispense with encouragement and recognition. Many things of permanent value have been created only because the creative individual received, at one time or another, a great deal of encouragement and stimulation. Yet, in the final analysis, he must rely on himself alone. Support and encouragement can be easily withdrawn and constitute only fragile crutches on the slippery creative terrain. The condition of self-sufficiency and self-responsibility has to be rooted within the creative person.

Give at least *five* reasons why it's good to be alone.

Here are examples of what some of the world's most respected thinkers and others have said about the subject:

1. The best thinking has been done in solitude. The worst has been done in turmoil.

   —THOMAS ALVA EDISON

2. Conversation enriches the understanding, but solitude is the school of genius.

   —EDWARD GIBBON

3. If you can only make it with people, and not alone, you can't make it.

   —CLARK E. MOUSTAKAS

4. The ability to be alone *with* yourself and to be self-energizing, self-stimulating and self-igniting—the ability to be either active or passive when alone but to know freedom from boredom and anxiety—at once makes you independent, self-reliant and thus a more mature, as well as an easier person with whom to have a relationship.

   —THEODORE ISAAC RUBIN

5. Loneliness is only an opportunity to cut adrift and find yourself.

   —ANNA MONROE

6. Solitude makes us tougher toward ourselves and tenderer toward others: in both ways it improves our character.

   —FRIEDRICH NIETZSCHE

7. If you're not able to communicate successfully between yourself and yourself, how are you supposed to make it with the strangers outside?

   —JULES FEIFFER

Real intelligence is a creative use of knowledge, not merely an accumulation of facts. The slow thinker who can finally come up with an idea of his own is more important to the world than a walking encyclopaedia who hasn't learned how to use the information productively.
KENNETH WINEBRENNER

Creative Memory

The unconscious is a vast storehouse of memories: facts, observations, impressions, ideas and associations. The creative individual's unconscious is always richly stocked with these, but this does not in itself indicate creative ability. Most of us know people who seem to have all kinds of information and facts at their fingertips, yet have never been able to achieve much in a creative way. Frequently the reason for this is that their memory functions as a rigidly ordered storehouse of deposited concepts, which precludes a flexible and imaginative use of them.

That a prodigious memory can act as a deterrent to creativity has been pointed out by scientist Ralph Gerard:

> Memory is a desirable attribute; but it is not worthwhile if, as is often the case, one pays for it by having a nervous system that somehow fixes so easily that it loses pliability and the ability to use facts in reasoning and imagining. The general experience has been that the memory wizards are likely to know everything but are not able to do much with it; they are not creative people. There are, of course, notable exceptions; if you happen to be a memory wizard you may also be creative, but the chances are strongly against it.

What makes memory creative is a state of flux or dynamic mobility in its components. The noncreative memory encapsulates or files its data and impressions neatly into independent groupings, clusterings and categories, all clearly bounded and demarcated. The creative memory, on the other hand, has permeability in its structural boundaries, so that all sorts of related or even unrelated data, impressions and concepts can be cross-indexed and interassociated. Furthermore, in the unconscious of the creative individual there is an incessant rearranging, pruning, discarding, relating, recombining and refining of ideas taking place. Such a permeably structured and dynamically fluid memory is hospitable to the formation of new combinations of ideas.

He who has imagination without learning,
has wings and no feet.
JOSEPH JOUBERT

Background of Fundamental Knowledge

In spite of the increasing contemporary trend toward specialization in almost every occupation and profession, the realization is growing that no specialist is able to make any significant contribution in his field of endeavor, unless he is well versed in many fields beyond his own particular specialization. Almost every field has evolved to such a high degree of complexity and difficulty that it takes continuous, unremitting study and learning in many diverse areas to be able to function creatively.

It has been estimated that it takes an average of only four to seven years after graduation for the intellectual baggage a person has accumulated during his educational career to become obsolete, unless he actively continues his education. It is also estimated that in certain technical fields as much as a third of a person's time during the working day has to be devoted to keeping up with the ever-increasing arsenal of new knowledge. And this accumulating information deals exclusively with the area of a person's specialty. For creative thinking, however, one needs competence that spans a great variety of disciplines. Heedful of this, the creative person makes education a vital part of his career design. His goal is to become intellectually broad without spreading himself thin, and deep without becoming pedantic.

One reason why the specialist (especially in technological fields) is frequently noncreative, is his inability to see beyond the accepted narrow area of his particular field of specialization. As William J. J. Gordon, founder of Synectics, Inc., has pointed out,

> Many highly trained people naturally tend to think in terms of the dogma of their own technology and it frightens them to

twist their conventions out of phase. Their conventions sometimes constitute a background of knowledge upon which they rely for their emotional stability. Such experts do not want cracks to appear. They identify their psychic order with the cosmic order and any cracks are signs of their orderly cosmos breaking up.

The narrow specialist frequently thinks he knows it all and takes inordinate pride in his expertise. When confronted with ideas or approaches that are somewhat unorthodox, he feels compelled to prove, often with convincing logic, that they just wouldn't work. The creative person with a more open mind and global grasp of things will often not accept or believe the arguments that the expert advances. He goes ahead, develops his own method of approach, and is frequently successful with problems considered by the expert to be insoluble.

Perhaps the chief danger of specialization is, however, that it emphasizes, even demands, strict conformity to the accepted and established dogmas and conventions of a field. Learning to comply with the established dogma starts early in a person's educational career. By the time he is ready to graduate into original production, he frequently finds that he is unable to unhook himself from its bondage. Relatively few individuals find the courage to tackle new problems in a new and unconventional manner; only a few transcend their subjugation to the traditional and jump ahead to original viewpoints and approaches.

This is not to gainsay the value of mastering the traditional methods and established canons of a field. Without mastery of the accumulated knowledge of a field—which takes an enormous amount of study and practice—one's compelling hunches remain mere flashes in the creative pan. The power of originating ideas without skill and knowledge often prevents their full exploitation. Still, the important point is that one cannot afford to be unduly influenced or enslaved by established knowledge. Creativity is and remains the natural enemy of dogma and conformity.

Ideas, like young wine, should be put in storage and taken up again only after they have been allowed to ferment and to ripen.
RICHARD STRAUSS

Incubation

There comes a time, during the creative process, when thinking gets ponderous and clogged, when errors start to pile up and no further new insights occur. This is the time when the creative person ceases his work on the problem and turns to something different and less confining. Many creative people find a welcome change of pace in music, painting, sightseeing, manual tasks, daydreaming, reverie, etc. These activities not only provide a refreshing interlude, but allow the unconscious mental processes freedom to operate unrestrained by conscious concentration.

Although the creative person spends a great deal of his conscious effort to solve a problem, he realizes the limitations of this effort and finally resorts to incubation. As psychologist John M. Schlien points out:

> Although he has confidence in his ability, the creative person also has an attitude of respect for the problem and admits the limits of his conscious power in forcing the problem to solution. At some point, called "incubation" by many who have reported the process, he treats the problem "as if it had a life of its own," which will, in its time and in its relation to his subliminal or autonomous thought processes, come to solution. He will consciously work on the problem, but there comes a point when he will "sleep on it."

The unconscious autonomous thought processes during the incubation period take over and continue solving the problem. And frequently, where the conscious forcing of the problem to solution failed, the incubatory process succeeds.

The philosopher, Bertrand Russell, provides an excellent example of the value of incubation:

Very gradually I have discovered ways of writing with a minimum of worry and anxiety. When I was young each fresh piece of serious work used to seem to me for a time—perhaps a long time—to be beyond my powers. I would fret myself into a nervous state from fear that it was never going to come right. I would make one unsatisfying attempt after another, and in the end have to discard them all. At last I found that such fumbling attempts were a waste of time. It appeared that after first contemplating a book on some subject, and after giving serious preliminary attention to it, I needed a period of subconscious incubation which would not be hurried and was if anything impeded by deliberate thinking. Sometimes I would find, after a time, that I had made a mistake, and that I could not write the book I had had in mind. But often I was more fortunate. Having, by a time of very intense concentration, planted the problem in my sub-consciousness, it would germinate underground until, suddenly, the solution emerged with blinding clarity, so that it only remained to write down what had appeared as if in a revelation.

> *Ideas are such funny things; they never*
> *work unless you do.*
> HERBERT V. PROCHNOW

Anticipation of Productive Periods

The creative person develops a *retrospective awareness* of the periods when he solved his problems creatively. He takes note of the methods that were successful and those that failed. He tries to learn why by retracing, as far as he can, the routes he followed and noting those he avoided. He has learned that knowledge of his particular idiosyncrasies and style of creating facilitates his creative process.

He schedules his creative thinking periods for times that are favorable for producing ideas. He is aware of his personal rhythms and peaks and valleys of output. By keeping a record of those periods during the day or night in which he is most creative, he can establish a pattern and plan ahead, reserving peak periods for concentration and uninhibited thinking, and his less productive time for reading and for gathering information. Even if he has not established a time sheet of productive periods, he has at least developed a sensitivity to those moods that promise really creative returns from his efforts, and he knows when they are approaching.

> *Any supreme insight is a metaphor.*
> H. PARKHURST

Ability to Think in Metaphors

Since antiquity, metaphor has been considered one of the most potent tools for the creative worker, irrespective of his field of specialization. Aristotle, for example, stated that "the greatest thing by far is to be the master of metaphor." He regarded metaphoric ability, which implies perception or discernment of linkages and qualitative similarities between disparate phenomena and objects, as a mark of genius.

In technology, science and problem solving in general, it is frequently metaphor that provides the key to a new invention, a new theory or a novel solution to a problem. Poetry, literature and art, of course, could not exist without metaphors, because only the metaphoric mode is able to communicate the deeper reality and relationships, the "qualitative kinships" that exist between things. Thus, any radically new perception or meaning, no matter what the field, tends to adopt a metaphoric expression.

Let us take, for example, the increasingly frequent use of visual metaphors in contemporary advertising. The visual metaphor in advertising relates the product or service to other objects, symbols or products, not literally or logically closely associated with it. This gives added new meaning to the product or service.

How and why does the visual metaphor have such a powerful impact in advertising?

Metaphor's arresting quality. An effective metaphoric ad is arresting in that it captures and compels attention. Its appeal and impact is directed to the reader's imagination rather than his reason. Because the metaphoric ad presents something new, which is at the same time unexplained, it acts as an instant spur to attention.

Metaphoric brevity and simplicity. Since almost everyone nowadays suffers from a surfeit of things clamoring for attention, as well as from acute shortage of time, brevity and simplicity have become two of our more pervasive needs.

One of the best devices for delivering an advertising message with brevity and directness is the metaphor. This is because a metaphor holds the several imputed characteristics, or attributes, of a product together in a single image. Rendered conceptually, these would frequently require a long-winded description. Furthermore, because the concise metaphoric image also carries subtle feeling overtones that are responsible for engaging the readers' interests and values, it can be called the "emotional shorthand" of advertising.

Comprehensive adequacy. Metaphor, in a sense, gives a fuller, more complete account of the product's image, or personality, than does a strictly literal, descriptive presentation. While a conceptual or descriptive presentation of sales points has, perhaps, greater precision than the metaphoric image, it leaves a feeling of incompleteness. The metaphoric ad, on the other hand, while apparently lacking in pinpointing precision, compensates for it through presenting the *extensive* product attributes in a single, concentrated *intensive* image.

The emotional power of metaphor. Metaphor seems to possess an emotional power which conceptual statements rarely have. This is mainly because the visual metaphor can associate the product with the reader's wants, needs, desires and values. At the same time that it heightens the reader's feelings about the product personality, it also abates his ever present attitudes of caution, skepticism and criticalness toward advertising claims.

The most important quality of metaphor, however, is its *evocative quality*: it evokes the experience or meaning from within the reader rather than describing what is on the outside. Metaphor gains access to the unconscious matrix where experiences, things and objects cohabit and commingle with each other in every degree of intimacy, like tangled branches of vines. Our conscious mind cannot, as a rule, "see" these kinships. For the purpose of recognition, the mind categorizes and differentiates objects and experiences into neat pigeon-holes. Only metaphor can communicate to us the qualitative relationships between things, relationships that are invisible to the conscious eye. And whenever there is a discovery of unsuspected kinships between things there is a feeling that frequently amounts to a "revelation."

Metaphor also draws to light the hidden mood of feelings and desires. Discursive or conceptual language in the realm of feelings is inadequate. Only through the expressive metaphor can the tremendous variety, nuances and shadings of feelings be elicited. And a feeling that translates itself into an idea is, as a rule, more effective than the reverse, especially in advertising.

Launching a new product or brand. Aside from the initial success of novelty, a new product or brand, when introduced to the public, often creates a conflict in the consumer's mind between the old brand(s) he habitually uses and the new brand vying for a place in the market. This conflict all too often ends in the victory of the average consumer's conservative tendency to stay with the familiar product, and this is especially the case when the new product fails to acquire a distinct image or personality with which the consumer could readily or willingly identify.

One of the most effective and rapid ways of creating a personality for a new product or brand is by linking the new brand metaphorically with an accepted, popular or established value or symbol. In order that the unknown new brand may acquire an identity, it must metaphorically "borrow" the attributes of something that is valued or appreciated. The most common metaphorical way of "grafting" an identity to a new product or brand which intrinsically has only an indeterminate personality, is to present it in combination with another product which is generically in a different product category.

Metaphor goes beyond the merely practical; it packs a force that ineluctably turns the reader to the experiential, to actually wanting to try the new brand. The metaphoric ad can help a new brand, first, to acquire, and then to transmit to readers its unique personality.

Revitalizing an old image. Through long-term reiteration of sales concepts, a product's personality frequently goes stale. It loses its punch and novelty and can become a source of irritation even to those consumers who are noted for their brand loyalty. This is the time when a novel metaphoric bridge to some new, hitherto unperceived, symbols or values can breathe new life into the product's personality and enliven its image.

A product displayed in metaphoric association with some other product, object or symbol becomes alive. It abounds in significance and swarms with new meanings. An ad's "aliveness" or vitality is frequently considered to be the measure of its merit, and rightly so, for no other term than "aliveness" is appropriate to describe one of the most essential characteristics of effective advertising. To a large measure, it is because of an ad's aliveness and vitality that it catches attention, arouses interest and sustained curiosity, and is remembered.

> *To be surrounded by beautiful things has*
> *much influence upon the human creature;*
> *to make beautiful things has more.*
> CHARLOTTE P. GILMAN

Aesthetic Orientation

Highly creative individuals in all fields have been noted for their strong aesthetic sensitivities and their love of the arts. This observation, gleaned from their biographies, remained rather incidental and anecdotal until it was experimentally substantiated by a group of behavioral scientists at the Institute of Personality Assessment and Research in Berkeley, California. Here, in the comfortable, homelike atmosphere of a converted fraternity house, a group of psychologists engaged in one of the most intensive and thorough studies of the creative individual undertaken anywhere in the world.

The procedure, which they termed "the living-in method of assessment," entailed bringing to the Institute groups of highly creative individuals for a period of several days, during which time they were subjected to countless batteries of psychological tests, personality scales, in-depth interviews and behavioral observations. Hundreds of creative individuals—architects, research scientists, inventors, engineers, mathematicians, artists and writers—nominated by their peers as the most highly original persons in their respective fields, have been studied by this method.

One of the instruments used was the highly respected *Study of Values Test* which measures the relative dominance of six basic interests and values: theoretical, economic, aesthetic, social, political and religious. The classification is based on the works of the brilliant psychologist Eduard Spranger, who maintained that the personalities of people are best known by the values they hold. The highly significant finding of this test was that the creative subjects from widely diverse fields all scored highest on the "aesthetic" and "theoretical" scales. These scores, in fact, were considerably higher than on the "political," "economic," "social" and "religious" scales.

Many creative individuals claim that openness to the aesthetic sense during the creative process enables them to arrive at a more dynamic and unique integration of the images and thoughts they use. In addition, it permits them to function with the greatest economy of time, energy and resources.

Several recent innovative workshop/seminars in the areas of management development, problem solving and decision making have made use of art-type experiences and activities—ranging from "painting a mess," doodling with colored pens, drawing human figures and landscapes, using modeling clay and making block designs, to interpreting films, listening to musical selections and creating poems. The rather astounding results obtained through these unorthodox methods, used with sober, practical, profit-oriented managers and executives in the business world, are that they all reported gains far surpassing those that are accomplished with the standard techniques used in management development and training. Art experiences, apparently even of a few days' duration, led these individuals to increased sensitivity, enhanced problem solving capacity, efficiency and a feeling of dynamic equilibrium and well-being.

Other Characteristics

Here are some of the other characteristics that differentiate the more creative individual from the less creative:

- He (or she) is more observant and perceptive, and puts a high value on independent "truth-to-oneself" perception. He perceives things the way other people do, but also the ways others do not.
- He is more independent in his judgments, and his self-directive behavior is determined by his own set of values and ethical standards.
- He balks at group standards, conformity pressures and external controls. He asserts his independence without being hostile or aggressive and he speaks his mind without being domineering. If necessary, he is flexible enough to simulate the prevailing norms of cultural and organizational behavior.
- He dislikes policing himself and others; he does not like to be bossed around. He can readily entertain impulses and ideas that are commonly considered taboo, or that break with convention. He has a spirit of adventure.
- He is highly individualistic and nonconventional in a constructive manner. Psychologist Donald W. MacKinnon

puts it this way: "Although independent in thought and action, the creative person does not make a show of his independence; he does not do the off-beat thing narcissistically, that is, to call attention to himself. . . . He is not a deliberate nonconformist but a genuinely independent and autonomous person."

- He has wide interests and multiple potentials—sufficient to succeed in several careers.
- He is constitutionally more energetic and vigorous and, when creatively engaged, can marshal an exceptional fund of psychic and physical energy.
- He is less anxious and possesses greater stability.
- His complex personality has, simultaneously, more primitive and more sophisticated, more destructive and more constructive, crazier and saner aspects. He has a greater appreciation and acceptance of the nonrational elements in himself and others.
- He is willing to entertain and express personal impulses, and pays more attention to his "inner voices." He likes to see himself as being different from others, and he has greater self-acceptance.
- He has strong aesthetic drive and sensitivity, and a greater interest in the artistic and aesthetic fields. He prefers to order the forms of his own experience aesthetically and the solutions he arrives at must not only be creative, but elegant. Truth for him has to be clothed in beauty to make it attractive.
- He searches for philosophical meanings and theoretical constructs and tends to prefer working with ideas, in contradistinction to the less creative who prefer to deal with the practical and concrete.
- He has a greater need for variety, and is almost insatiable for intellectual ordering and comprehension.
- He places great value on humor of the philosophical sort, and possesses a unique sense of humor.
- He regards authority as arbitrary, contingent on continued and demonstrable superiority. He separates source

from content when valuating communications; judges and reaches conclusions on the basis of the information itself, and not on whether the information source was an "authority" or an "expert."

STOP

Ponder and practice all that you've learned so far and try the following C.Q. inventories to see if you really "measure up" to the full range of your creative potential.

PART IV
Post-Test

VALUE ORIENTATIONS

A = Agree
B = In-between or Don't know
C = Disagree

1. Conservative values are necessary for stability. _____
2. I have attained a clear perspective on my life. _____
3. I have a resigned, nonenthusiastic approach to life. _____
4. I fear the disappearance of my appetite for life more than I fear death. _____
5. I feel that life is a journey in which adventure plays an important role. _____
6. I find politics boring. _____
7. I feel that the adage "Do unto others . . ." is more important than "To thine own self be true." _____
8. To be a participant in life is more important than to be an observer. _____
9. I am quite idealistic. _____
10. I think that those who take life as an adventure are reckless. _____
11. I feel that I have a liberal social outlook. _____
12. I aspire to achieve a lot in life. _____
13. As I grow older, my appetite for life is diminishing. _____
14. Finding meaning and consummation in my life now is far more important than a happy life after death. _____
15. I see little point in extraverted sociability or self-sacrifice for social causes. _____

16. I feel that my life is far too short to permit me to do all I want to do or might do. _____
17. The "truth" that I perceive is shaped according to my values. _____
18. The adage, "Enjoy life to its fullest," has been more significant in my life than "Seek self-fulfill-ment." _____

Circle and add up the values for each item.

	A	B	C		A	B	C
1.	−1	0	+1	10.	−1	0	+1
2.	−1	0	+1	11.	+1	0	−1
3.	−2	0	+2	12.	+1	0	−1
4.	+2	0	−2	13.	−1	0	+1
5.	+1	0	−1	14.	+1	0	−1
6.	+1	0	−1	15.	+1	0	−1
7.	−1	0	+1	16.	+2	0	−2
8.	0	+2	0	17.	+2	0	−2
9.	+1	0	−1	18.	−2	0	+2

YOUR SUBSCORE:

ATTITUDES TOWARD WORK

A = Agree
B = In-between or Don't know
C = Disagree

1. I enjoy work in which I must constantly keep trying out new approaches and possibilities. _____
2. When I have completed a piece of work, I like to be freed of it. _____
3. While working at one project, I often think of the next one I want to tackle. _____
4. Financial success is my predominant motivation. _____
5. I prefer to brainstorm in a group rather than alone. _____
6. I tend to get disturbed if I'm not praised for my good work. _____
7. To be regarded as a good team member is important to me. _____
8. People who are theory-oriented are less important than are those who are practical. _____
9. I believe that creativity is restricted to specialized fields of endeavor. _____
10. To be efficient, one must try to keep regular hours and maintain an organized work pattern. _____
11. I find it easy to identify flaws in the ideas of others. _____
12. I am much more interested in coming up with new ideas than I am in trying to sell them to others. _____
13. I am constantly either finding or seeking challenging problems to solve. _____

14. I have never experienced being "consumed" by my work. _____

15. I seek to learn ways to promote greater productivity in myself. _____

16. I feel somewhat apprehensive when taking on a new job. _____

17. New ideas have to have some value or worth to be called creative. _____

18 I find that I cannot work intently on a problem for more than an hour or two at a stretch. _____

19. I would prefer to work in an atmosphere of strict competition rather than one of strict cooperation. _____

20. I don't like to work under pressure. _____

21. I feel that hard work is one of the basic factors of success. _____

22. I am able to work over extended periods of time, frequently to the point of exhaustion. _____

23. A theory, to be good at all, has to have a practical application. _____

24. I find that I have more problems than I can tackle, more work than there is time for. _____

25. I tend not to be too painstaking or disciplined in my work. _____

26. In my work I don't like to proceed unless the instructions are made clear to me. _____

27. I am more likely than most people to see my future career largely within the boundaries of my organization and to be concerned chiefly with its problems and with my promotion within it. _____

28. I feel that I may have a special contribution to give to the world. _____

Circle and add up the values for each item.

	A	B	C		A	B	C
1.	+1	0	−1	5.	−1	0	+1
2.	+1	0	−1	6.	−1	0	+1
3.	+1	0	−1	7.	0	+1	0
4.	−1	0	+1	8.	−1	0	+1

	A	B	C			A	B	C
9.	−1	0	+1		19.	0	+2	+1
10.	+1	+2	0		20.	−1	+1	0
11.	−1	+1	0		21.	+1	+2	0
12.	+2	+1	0		22.	+1	0	−1
13.	+2	0	−2		23.	−1	0	+1
14.	−1	0	+1		24.	+1	0	−1
15.	+1	0	−1		25.	−1	0	+1
16.	−1	0	+1		26.	−1	0	+1
17.	0	+1	0		27.	−2	0	+2
18.	−1	0	+1		28.	+1	0	−1

YOUR SUBSCORE:

PROBLEM SOLVING BEHAVIORS

A = Agree
B = In-between or Don't know
C = Disagree

1. Only fuzzy thinkers resort to metaphors and analogies. _____
2. Adults who become childishly involved with things are immature. _____
3. I am able to concentrate to a degree where I become oblivious to everything else. _____
4. I sometimes stay up all night when I'm doing something that interests me. _____
5. Some of the penetrating insights I have experienced have been touched off by trivial or insignificant coincidences. _____
6. I think the statement, "ideas are a dime a dozen," hits the nail on the head. _____
7. Problems that do not have clear-cut and unambiguous answers have very little interest for me. _____
8. I rely on intuitive hunches and the feeling of "rightness" or "wrongness" when moving toward the solution of a problem. _____
9. I enjoy aesthetic and sensuous impressions. _____
10. I am a reflective thinker. _____
11. When faced with a problem, I usually investigate and consider a wide variety of approaches. _____
12. I rather enjoy fooling around with new ideas, even if there is no practical payoff. _____

13. I get a feeling of excitement when an idea I am working on begins to jell. _____

14. I sometimes experience a flood of ideas—far more than I can immediately capture or use. _____

15. I believe that one should always "sleep on a problem." _____

16. I believe that indulging in daydreams and fantasy is a waste of time. _____

17. I am frequently haunted by my problems and cannot let go of them. _____

18. I am more intrigued by complex problems than by simple and easily understood problems. _____

19. When thinking about a problem, I have an exceptional ability to shift gears, to adopt new viewpoints, to discard one frame of reference for another. _____

20. The work that goes on at unconscious levels is often more important in solving problems than what is done consciously. _____

21. I enjoy playing around with the materials I use in my work. _____

22 Harmony of form and function, means and ends, dominate the way I do my work. _____

23. I enjoy acting on a hunch just to see what will happen. _____

24. I can think of more unusual, more unique solutions to problems than can most other people. _____

25. I enjoy the "aha" moments of sudden insight into things. _____

26. I have more capacity than the average person to tolerate ambiguity. _____

27. A painstaking, disciplined effort is mandatory in creative problem solving. _____

28. There are times when I experience a heightened awareness, a capacity to see more, hear more, sense more than is usual for me. _____

Circle and add up the values for each item.

	A	B	C		A	B	C
1.	−2	0	+2	15.	+1	+2	0
2.	−1	0	+1	16.	−2	0	+2
3.	+2	0	−2	17.	+1	0	−1
4.	+1	0	−1	18.	+1	0	−1
5.	+1	0	−1	19.	+2	0	−2
6.	−1	+2	+1	20.	+2	0	−2
7.	−1	0	+1	21.	+1	0	−1
8.	+2	0	−2	22.	+1	0	−1
9.	+2	0	−2	23.	+1	0	−1
10.	+2	0	−2	24.	+2	0	−2
11.	+2	0	−2	25.	+2	0	−2
12.	+1	0	−1	26.	+2	0	−2
13.	+1	0	−1	27.	+1	+2	0
14.	+1	0	−1	28.	+2	0	−2

YOUR SUBSCORE:

CHILDHOOD-ADOLESCENCE

A = Agree
B = In-between or Don't know
C = Disagree

1. I wasn't particularly imaginative up to the age of ten. _____

2. I was not very ambitious during my adolescence. _____

3. One or both of my parents had many unorthodox and unconventional ideas. _____

4. One of my parents was always involved in several hobbies or handicrafts. _____

5. During my childhood and adolescence my mother gave me practically all the freedom I wanted. _____

6. My parents considered education nice to have but not necessary. _____

7. During my youth my friends were not very achievement oriented. _____

8. Compared to others, I didn't do much reading (excluding schoolwork) between the ages of twelve and eighteen. _____

9. During my adolescence I rarely had a desire to be alone to pursue my own interests and thoughts. _____

10. Throughout my education, I had many part-time jobs. _____

Circle and add up the values for each item.

	A	B	C			A	B	C
1.	−2	0	+2		6.	−1	0	+1
2.	−1	0	+1		7.	−1	0	+1
3.	+1	0	−1		8.	−1	0	+1
4.	+1	0	−1		9.	−1	0	+1
5.	+1	0	−1		10.	+1	0	−1

YOUR SUBSCORE:

INTERESTS

A = Agree
B = In-between or Don't know
C = Disagree

1. I am more impressed with what I don't know than with what I do know. _____
2. I wouldn't mind living and working in a foreign country. _____
3. I wouldn't mind having a career that involved much traveling. _____
4. My interests are broad. _____
5. I would rather be a congressman than a philosopher. _____
6. If I had to choose between two occupations other than the one I now have, I would rather be a physician than an explorer. _____
7. In my work I have attempted to follow in the footsteps of a man (or woman) I admire. _____
8. I like to attend concerts. _____
9. Some of my hobbies would be considered "offbeat." _____
10. I wouldn't mind being hypnotized. _____
11. I have always been active in creative pursuits. _____
12. I prefer to learn things in my own way rather than rely on books. _____
13. I like modern art. _____
14. I don't enjoy going to museums. _____
15. Perfect balance and order are absolutely necessary for a good composition. _____
16. I never choke up or sob when watching a movie. _____

17. I like to play with children. _____
18. I pretty well know what I will be doing ten years from now. _____

Circle and add up the values for each item.

	A	B	C			A	B	C
1.	+1	0	−1		10.	+1	+2	0
2.	+1	0	−1		11.	+1	0	−1
3.	+1	0	−1		12.	+1	0	−1
4.	+1	0	−1		13.	+1	+2	0
5.	−1	0	+1		14.	−1	0	+2
6.	−1	0	+1		15.	−1	0	+2
7.	+1	+2	0		16.	−1	0	+1
8.	+1	0	−1		17.	+1	0	−1
9.	+1	0	−1		18.	+1	0	−1

YOUR SUBSCORE:

INTERPERSONAL RELATIONS

A = Agree
B = In-between or Don't know
C = Disagree

1. I tend to take the initiative in social situations. _____
2. I am apt to drop something I want to do when others feel that it isn't worth doing. _____
3. I am usually quite outspoken in my opinions. _____
4. I know how to listen to what lies behind a person's words. _____
5. I tend to get annoyed when someone delays me. _____
6. I tend to get disturbed if I'm not accepted, or listened to, at a party. _____
7. People who make it easy for others to understand them are foolish. _____
8. I like to keep up with the latest clothing styles. _____
9. Compared to most people, I need more social interaction and have a keener interest in interpersonal relationships. _____
10. I do not much care what others think of me. _____
11. Conversation at many parties tends to annoy me because of its superficiality. _____
12. I place a greater value on humor than do most other people. _____
13. In dealing with people, it is more important to be diplomatic than open and direct. _____
14. I sometimes pretend to be other than I am, so people will like me. _____
15. I am usually able to win other people over to my point of view. _____

16. It is more important for me to do what I believe to be right than to try to win the approval of others. _____

17. People often tell me their personal problems. _____

18. My own feelings and ideas do not stimulate me as much as do outside events and incidents. _____

19. I always try to be kind, warm and understanding with people. _____

20. I don't hesitate to ask others to help me to clarify my own problems. _____

21. People feel that I trust them and that they can trust me. _____

22. I am curious about the values that hold other people's lives together. _____

23. People who claim to understand a great deal without being told live in a fool's paradise. _____

24. I don't like to express strong approval or disapproval of the behavior of others. _____

25. I frequently make concessions to avoid unpleasant situations. _____

26. Provided I had the skills, I would rather spend an evening building some new furniture in the workshop than playing cards with a neighbor and his wife. _____

27. I seldom take the trouble to discover how things look from another person's point of view. _____

28. I tend to act on the assumption that people want to do the good and fulfilling thing. _____

29. I do the best I can to get the attention and admiration I deserve. _____

30. I frequently feel that my opinion is more valid than is the majority opinion. _____

31. I really don't mind if people disagree with me. _____

32. I am more apt than most people to stick to my point of view when I find myself in disagreement with others. _____

Circle and add up the values for each item.

	A	B	C		A	B	C
1.	0	+2	+1	17.	+1	+2	0
2.	−1	0	+1	18.	−1	0	+1
3.	+1	0	−1	19.	+1	+2	0
4.	+1	0	−1	20.	+1	+2	0
5.	+1	0	−1	21.	+1	0	−1
6.	−1	+1	0	22.	+1	0	−1
7.	−1	0	+1	23.	−1	0	+2
8.	−1	0	+1	24.	+1	+2	0
9.	−1	+1	0	25.	−1	0	+1
10.	+1	+2	0	26.	+1	0	−1
11.	+1	0	−1	27.	−1	0	+1
12.	+1	0	−1	28.	+1	0	−1
13.	−1	+2	+1	29.	−1	0	+1
14.	−1	0	+1	30.	+1	0	−1
15.	+1	+2	0	31.	+1	+2	0
16.	+1	0	−1	32.	+1	+2	0

YOUR SUBSCORE:

PERSONALITY DIMENSIONS

A = Agree
B = In-between or Don't know
C = Disagree

1. I have never experienced failure. _____
2. I am more self-assertive than most people. _____
3. It is important for me to have a place for everything and everything in its place. _____
4. More than other people I need to have things interesting and exciting. _____
5. On occasion I can become childishly enthusiastic about an apparently simple thing. _____
6. A person needs to pat himself on the back a little now and then. _____
7. I am not always confident of my intellectual ability. _____
8. I avoid activities that are a little frightening. _____
9. I don't enjoy situations in which I can't know exactly what is going to happen. _____
10. I have more capacity to tolerate frustration than does the average person. _____
11. The sensuous quality of an experience is as important as is its intellectual quality. _____
12. I often observe myself almost as though I were someone else. _____
13. I often become moody and irritable when my thinking about a work in progress gets cloudy and confused. _____
14. I am a thoroughly dependable and responsible person. _____

15. I like people who follow the rule "business before pleasure." _____

16. If I were stranded in a strange city with neither friends, acquaintances, nor money, I think I would cope quite well. _____

17. The peak moments of my life often occur when I'm totally alone. _____

18. I am more objective than most people. _____

19. I am suspicious of people who do something nice for me. _____

20. I tend to do the things that are expected of me. _____

21. I feel I have tapped all my powers and talents. _____

22. I prefer the completed and polished over the unfinished and imperfect. _____

23. I am able to both participate in and observe my experiences. _____

24. I am curious about more things than are most people. _____

25. I don't mind suffering if it is for the sake of my growth and development. _____

26. I would rather be known as a reliable than as an imaginative person. _____

27. People who become intense in their feelings and expressions are somewhat unbalanced. _____

28. It is better to take things as they are and not probe too deeply into one's own or other people's feelings. _____

29. I'm curious to know how things fit together. _____

30. Some of my friends and acquaintances think that my ideas are impractical and offbeat, if not completely wild. _____

31. I like people who are spontaneous. _____

32. I sometimes get a kick out of breaking the rules and doing things I'm not supposed to do. _____

33. When someone tries to get ahead of me in a line of people, I usually point it out to him. _____

34. I frequently seem to surprise people with what I say. _____

35. I am more open to my feelings and emotions than are most people. _____

36. I regard myself to be a well-adjusted person. _____

37. I'm afraid of being laughed at. _____

38. I would enjoy spending an entire day alone, just "chewing the mental cud." _____

39. At times I have so enjoyed the ingenuity of a crook that I hoped he would go scot-free. _____

40. I tend to become upset if I cannot immediately come to a decision. _____

41. I feel I have capacities that have not yet been tapped. _____

42. More than most people, I sometimes feel lonely and apart, with a sense of mission that isolates me, in my own mind, from the average concerns of average men. _____

43. When under stress, I become confused and disorganized. _____

44. I am more critical than most people. _____

45. I place a great value on my psychological freedom. _____

46. I am freer of restraint and inhibitions than most people I know. _____

47. I like to take a playful approach even to things most people consider serious. _____

48. Know-how is more important than know-why. _____

Circle and add up the values for each item.

	A	B	C		A	B	C
1.	−2	0	+2	15.	−1	0	+1
2.	0	+2	0	16.	+1	0	−1
3.	−1	0	+1	17.	+1	0	−1
4.	+1	0	−1	18.	−1	0	+1
5.	+2	0	−2	19.	−1	0	+1
6.	+1	0	−1	20.	−1	0	+1
7.	−1	+1	0	21.	−1	0	+1
8.	−1	0	+1	22.	−1	0	+1
9.	−1	0	+1	23.	+2	0	−2
10.	+1	0	−1	24.	+2	0	−2
11.	+1	0	−1	25.	+1	0	−1
12.	+1	0	−1	26.	−1	0	+1
13.	+1	0	−1	27.	−1	0	+1
14.	0	+1	0	28.	−1	0	+1

	A	B	C		A	B	C
29.	+1	0	−1	39.	+1	0	−1
30.	+1	0	−1	40.	−1	0	+1
31.	+1	0	−1	41.	+1	0	−1
32.	+1	0	−1	42.	+1	0	−1
33.	+1	0	−1	43.	−1	+1	0
34.	+1	0	−1	44.	−1	0	+1
35.	+1	0	−1	45.	+2	0	−2
36.	0	+1	0	46.	+1	0	−1
37.	−1	0	+1	47.	+1	0	−1
38.	+2	0	−2	48.	−1	0	+1

YOUR SUBSCORE:

SELF-PERCEPTION CHECKLIST

Below is a list of adjectives and terms that describe people. Indicate with a check mark *twelve* words that best characterize you.

_____ sensitive		_____ a self-starter
_____ daring		_____ individualistic
_____ competitive		_____ restless
_____ witty		_____ thoughtful
_____ effective		_____ rigid
_____ dependable		_____ ingenious
_____ unassuming		_____ serious-minded
_____ gracious		_____ idealistic
_____ persistent		_____ reserved
_____ warm		_____ intelligent
_____ reflective		_____ frank
_____ versatile		_____ cooperative
_____ punctual		_____ committed
_____ interests wide		_____ orderly
_____ intuitive		_____ unexcitable
_____ diplomatic		_____ impulsive
_____ reliable		_____ different
_____ logical		_____ cheerful
_____ mischievous		_____ dominant
_____ retiring		_____ ambitious
_____ meek		_____ determined
_____ considerate		_____ self-denying
_____ imaginative		_____ orthodox
_____ contented		_____ excitable
_____ moody		_____ industrious
_____ capable		_____ stimulating

_____ loyal   _____ attractive
_____ conservative   _____ congenial

The following have values of +2:

daring   imaginative
persistent   a self-starter
reflective   individualistic
versatile   ingenious
interests wide   committed
intuitive   ambitious

The following have values of +1:

sensitive   intelligent
witty   impulsive
effective   different
mischievous   determined
moody   excitable
capable   industrious
restless   stimulating
idealistic

The rest have values of 0.

Add up the values for each item.

YOUR SUBSCORE:

NEGATIVE SELF-IMAGES

Following is a list of relatively *negative* terms that are used to describe people. Indicate with a check mark the one term of each pair that is closest to describing you, or is less offensive to your self-image. Remember, even if neither term really describes you, select the one of each pair that is nearest to what conceivably could be your negative trait. Be sure to check one of *each* pair of choices.

1. _____Inflexible
   _____Unrealistic
2. _____Fearful
   _____Hostile
3. _____Shrewd
   _____Rebellious
4. _____Inhibited
   _____Flighty
5. _____Cunning
   _____Radical
6. _____Eccentric
   _____Egotistical
7. _____Aloof
   _____Conventional
8. _____Disorganized
   _____Indifferent
9. _____Orthodox
   _____Excitable
10. _____Judgmental
    _____Disorderly

11. _____Bohemian
    _____Aggressive
12. _____Destructive
    _____Phony
13. _____Immature
    _____Selfish
14. _____Restless
    _____Overcritical
15. _____Unfulfilled
    _____Exhibitionistic
16. _____Emotional
    _____Unsure
17. _____Cynical
    _____Long-suffering
18. _____Vain
    _____Odd
19. _____Slow
    _____Dependent
20. _____Timid
    _____Closed-minded

To obtain your score, count how many of the following traits were checked:

1.	Unrealistic____		11.	Bohemian____
2.	Hostile____		12.	Destructive____
3.	Rebellious____		13.	Immature____
4.	Flighty____		14.	Restless____
5.	Radical____		15.	Unfulfilled____
6.	Eccentric____		16.	Emotional____
7.	Aloof____		17.	Cynical____
8.	Disorganized____		18.	Odd____
9.	Excitable____		19.	Slow____
10.	Disorderly____		20.	Timid____

YOUR SUBSCORE:

To compute your total score, add up your nine sub-scores.

Your Total Score

223–278	Exceptionally Creative
143–222	Very Creative
62–142	Above Average
34–61	Average
–6–33	Below Average
–185– –5	Noncreative

Politics is the science of who gets what,
when, and why.
SIDNEY HILLMAN

Power corrupts, but lack of power
corrupts absolutely.
ADLAI E. STEVENSON

The first and great commandment is,
"Don't let them scare you!"
ELMER DAVIS

PART V

Creativity at Work:
The Politics of
Selling Ideas

EVEN IF ONE has the ability to produce potentially good ideas, there is always the problem of convincing others that our ideas are valid and useful. Sometimes this takes greater creative effort than originating the idea itself. Indeed, it has been said that "an innovator is not successful (and perhaps not even innovative) until he puts his idea across to potential users and gains both acceptance and use for the product of his thought."

Why are many valuable ideas never implemented? Why do they stay locked up in people's minds? They do so because many people experience inordinate difficulty in promoting or "selling" ideas to others. Frequently, the cause of this problem is the fear of rebuff: it is a very universal and very human tendency to fear rejection, to fear being turned down. This fear may or may not be based on, or reinforced by, past failures at idea selling, or by past rejections that may have been either premature or unduly severe. Most of us tend to identify ourselves closely with our ideas, and a rejection of them is frequently interpreted as a personal slight, or a rejection of ourselves. Our ideas often tend to become extensions of our egos.

Another reason why many potentially useful ideas are never successfully prosecuted stems from a reluctance to face up to the difficult and time-consuming task of putting ideas into salable shape. Or it may be that the additional effort to convince others of the value of an idea somehow seems much less important than having conceived the idea in the first place. Many creative individuals have the mistaken notion that having an idea is the be all and end all of the creative process. They do not realize that the creative process does not end with an idea: it starts with an idea. Indeed, a person who comes up with brilliant ideas may have no advantage over the person who has no ideas—unless he or she knows how to present and sell them.

Ideas can rarely be sold and implemented in organizations without the support of key decision makers. A scientist or an engineer, for example, usually needs the support and backing of several managers or executives. A marketing specialist who wants to launch a new product idea, will need the backing and decisions of managers and peers in production and sales. In each case the crucial aspect of the situation is what effect your idea will have on the power structure in the organization. This means that you have to assess the wants and needs of those in power and how these relate to what your idea is trying to accomplish.

Have you ever come up with a brilliant proposal only to have it lost in the organizational shuffle? Have you ever proposed a new idea only to have your boss take credit for it? Has someone ever goofed-up in the implementation phases of your idea and somehow engineered it so you got the blame?

These and other similar incidents of organizational life have given a bad case of the blues to many a high achiever.

If you have been puzzled or even outraged by these or other operations of organizational politics and didn't know how to cope with them, perhaps your attitudes toward power are unrealistic.

Most people, if asked how power oriented they are, would modestly say they are not power oriented at all. Perhaps that is what you believe of yourself. Yet this may or may not be true.

All of us have an attitude toward power whether or not we are aware of it. Power is such a universal phenomenon that it is nearly as invisible as the air we breathe. And it isn't until our attention is focused on breathing or on power that we notice it. A saying that has its parallel to our power awareness is, "A fish would be the last living creature to discover water."

Almost everyone exercises power and is protective of the power he or she possesses. Human beings expend a great deal of time and energy to maintain and expand their power prerogatives. You do not have to make any value judgments about the relative merits of politics and power, but if you do not confront these squarely as facts of organizational life, your success rate at introducing new ideas is going to be poor, at best. To augment the chances of your idea's acceptance, you have to be especially sensitive to the political matrix in your organization. If you are not a natural at handling power, or if you feel some aversion toward it, then it behooves you to enlist the aid of others who can help you to get your idea across in the face of any possible political resistance.

There are two basic considerations about selling ideas that are often overlooked by many intelligent people. First, to be adept at selling ideas, one needs a cluster of skills labeled "assertive skills" by some and "selling" or "political skills" by others. Whatever the label, these skills involve both the willingness and the ability to push your idea and to persist in advancing it until you have gained acceptance. Second, it is a hard, prickly fact that ideas are more upsetting of the status quo than people realize. Abstractly viewed, "an idea is simply an idea," but an idea is also a device that poses a threat to those in positions of power.

Everyday words in our vocabulary serve well to describe the behavior of those aggressors we interact with routinely: one-upmanship, put-downs, gamesmanship, intimidation, top dog, manipulation, elitism, domineeringness and spitefulness. At the other end of the scale our vocabulary is equally descriptive with terms like underdog, submissive, passive, mild-mannered, self-effacing, dependent, withdrawn and shy.

In the middle we find assertive, active, considerate, courteous, competitive, self-assured and forceful to describe the person who, while facile in coping with power, avoids extremes in either direction. Whatever the form of competition, the winners are usually found among the nonabrasively assertive members of the organization who display most clearly the other characteristics listed above. According to psychologist Abraham H. Maslow, people in this middle group are frequently and unjustly lumped with the aggressive, power-hungry types whose exalted ego level requires minute-by-minute confirmation. As he puts it, "High-dominance feeling should not be confused with domineeringness. The high-dominance personality is not necessarily a nasty person. High-dominance feeling implies self-confidence rather than aggressiveness."

Assertive-dominant persons possess many other characteristics. They:

- Are able to maintain a high level of thrust in promoting and implementing their ideas.
- Exhibit free-flowing, high-level energy even in creative leisure-time pursuits and activities.
- Have courage, creative vision and an unusual ability to overcome failures and roll with the punches.
- Have strong self-respect and feelings of mastery to handle challenging problems and a diversity of personalities.

- Are imperturbable and untroubled by the prospect of a confrontation, but seldom initiate or seek it out.
- Are able to signal their claim to rank by initiating their own choice and definition of a situation. They frequently set the tone of a gathering or meeting and define its limits and objectives.
- Are allowed the most talking time in problem solving meetings and are able to command all the attention they want or need. Their idea contributions receive more than average consideration, and the most significant points and remarks are usually addressed to them.
- Evince an air of self-assurance in an upright carriage, and they tend to hold their heads slightly higher than do less assertive-dominant persons.
- Exhibit an air of relaxation, a free unrestrained movement of the body, with arms swinging freely at their sides when walking.
- Have a penetrating but unself-conscious gaze.
- Behave courteously toward everyone and considerately toward those who are not adept at defending their ideas, or who feel they are down. They are ready to protect vulnerable subordinates.
- Are able to flexibly choose to adopt any of several "masks," rather than perpetually wearing the same face. They feel no compulsion to follow approved scripts, and are freer than others to experiment, ad lib, innovate and break new ground in unfamiliar situations.

POWER QUESTIONNAIRE

Here's your chance to discover your attitude toward power: do you rate as passive, assertive or aggressive?
Place a check in the appropriate column.

TRUE FALSE

1. Keeping the boss happy takes priority over the ability to come up with good ideas. ___ ___
2. "Everywhere I look, I see the Will to Power." ___ ___
3. Courtesy is one of the most effective tools for getting ahead. ___ ___
4. Power and politics are the keystones of most organizational results. ___ ___
5. One of the most important attributes a supervisor needs to make things work is fairness to subordinates. ___ ___
6. In a fair organization, the most creative persons will succeed and get ahead. ___ ___
7. It is necessary and effective to criticize subordinates for their mistakes. ___ ___
8. "Packaging" my ideas to get around people's prejudices would be distorting the idea and be a "sellout" of my integrity. ___ ___
9. Being cordial to important people, even if one doesn't like them, is as important as being good at creating new ideas. ___ ___
10. I shouldn't have to curry favor to get people to cooperate with me on my ideas or to do the job they are paid to do. ___ ___

To obtain your score, add up the values.

1.	T = 1;	F = 0		6.	T = 0;	F = 1
2.	T = 1;	F = 0		7.	T = 1;	F = 0
3.	T = 1;	F = 0		8.	T = 0;	F = 1
4.	T = 1;	F = 0		9.	T = 1;	F = 0
5.	T = 0;	F = 1		10.	T = 0;	F = 1

Analysis: If you scored 0 to 3 your view of power could be very naive. People probably take advantage of you quite frequently. Possibly you rationalize or forgive offenses done to you by others. You tend to cooperate with people even when you strongly disagree with what is done to your original idea.

A score of 8 to 10 shows you are extremely power oriented in your dealings with others. Chances are you are abrasive in your use of power and tolerate little or no pressure from others to change your ideas without fighting back. You are also likely to turn an ordinary problem into an unnecessary confrontation for the pleasure of winning your point at the expense of another person's ego. You tend to feel that there are no "win-win" situations and that one person's success at putting an idea across always involves another person's subordination.

A score of 4 to 7 is the assertive happy medium. You show flexibility in your use of power: sometimes you will use it; at other times, you won't, depending on how you read the situation. You are likely to be either flexibly cooperative or quietly competitive with your ideas, depending on the situational demands. Extreme scores at either end of the scale indicate either a tendency toward a reflexive withdrawal or a robust aggressiveness regardless of what might be needed to produce an effective outcome for your proposal.

Let's examine the answers in more detail.

1. *Keeping the boss happy takes priority over the ability to come up with good ideas.*

True: One of the most noticeable facts of organizational

life is that any time differences of opinion about an idea emerge between a boss and a subordinate, the odds are that the boss's opinion will prevail. This has nothing to do with "right" or "wrong" in any objective or moral sense. If the subordinate cannot persuade the superior, usually the best course of action is to drop the idea. When there are serious differences, the boss invariably wins—not because he is right, but because he is the boss. Your rating along the passive, assertive, aggressive continuum determines how you view your relationship with your boss.

Passive individuals often feel the boss isn't "fair" when he acts in a way that seems arbitrary. Often this serves as a rationalization for the person who doesn't have the persuasive and assertive skills needed to cope with the boss and the power of his higher rank. Passive individuals often feel a good idea or the right view on an issue ought to be judged on its merits. But the boss frequently has information that he cannot share, and the subordinates, not being able to share this information, disagree with his decisions.

The assertive person tends to take for granted the boss's authority and works his way around it to persuade the boss to his own point of view. The assertive person knows that the odds of getting his ideas across are contingent upon getting them past the boss's need to express his authority. He packages his ideas or proposals in such a way that they will appear to enhance the boss's prospects and stature.

The overly aggressive person may offend the boss by telling him he is wrong. The aggressive person usually confronts the boss whether or not it is the effective thing to do. Sometimes this brazen aggressiveness so disarms the boss that the individual gets away with it. Such a relationship, for as long as it lasts, is likely to be as ragged as a battle flag. Over the long run the less aggressive people in the organization are likely to come to the aid of the boss and form cliques to block the aggressive person. They may try to sabotage him by withholding crucial information or help when he needs it to further his ideas and his upward mobility.

2. *"Everywhere I look, I see the Will to Power."*

True: At least it was true for the philosopher Friedrich Nietzsche, whose words these are. He, like the philosopher Arthur Schopenhauer and the psychologist Alfred Adler, felt that the power motive is the most fundamental urge in human nature. All three felt that power, politics and the pursuit of higher position in hierarchies explain the bulk of human behavior and motivation.

Scientific research done by the Danish zoologist Thorleif Schieldorup-Ebbe in 1913 revealed that the lowly barnyard chicken belongs to an organizational structure in which one chicken at the top can express its dominance with impunity by pecking any other chicken. Subordinate chickens of the next level can peck those chickens of lower rank but cannot peck the boss chicken, and so on down the hierarchy, each level being allowed to peck lesser ranking chickens but not those of higher rank. In human terms, maintaining one's place in the pecking order is known as power or office politics.

Many people are not aware of the fact that humans form pecking orders just as naturally as chickens, or any other species of hierarchically arranged social animals. Somehow our culture has developed blind spots about social hierarchies and the accompanying facts of politics and power in organizations. The root of organizational politics, then, is the pecking order.

To be sure, not every human being is a born status seeker. Several recent studies have shown that many subordinates in hierarchical organizational structures accept their subordinate positions quite willingly. Far from gunning for, or challenging their superiors' positions, submissive persons like to look up to and admire their bosses. And this might well be to the good. If every subordinate was permanently on the alert to step into his superior's shoes at the first available opportunity, and if every boss had to remain constantly vigilant against usurpation of his or her power, the organization would run a genuine risk of disintegrating altogether.

3. *Courtesy is one of the most effective tools for getting ahead.*

True: Courtesy can be defined as the act of making others feel good or powerful in relationship to the pecking order. Courtesy is saying or doing things that keep people from feeling "put down." It reinforces their self-esteem in the context of the organization they share, whether it is comprised of two people or is a giant conglomerate.

Courtesy is simply the grease that lubricates the social order. While dominant individuals selectively use discourtesy to discombobulate rivals—as Lord Chesterton said: "A gentleman is never unintentionally rude"—discourteous bumpkins seldom go far up the hierarchy.

A "phony" is an aggressive person pretending not to be aggressive. His use of flattery and courtesy is transparently designed to serve his own purposes. Yet many people are unprepared to cope with the "phony" person. By avoiding him they often simply provide him the latitude to carry on the charade, much to their own chagrin. Many submissive people are better able to spot phonies than are the more assertive rivals of the phony.

It should be noted that people whose power needs are satisfied, who are generally respected and looked up to, are naturally courteous. They also derive greater enjoyment from their interpersonal relationships than do those individuals who occupy a lower position on the submissive-dominance scale.

4. *Power and politics are the keystones of most organizational results.*

True: The organizational pyramid or pecking order is the most pervasive and dominant fact of organizational life. Hierarchical arrangements of people, as represented by the organizational chart, are necessary for ideas to be implemented and work to be accomplished. As a species, we form social hierarchies spontaneously. Someone must be in charge before anything can even be started.

Politics, or the art of maneuvering for a better place in the hierarchy, is usually frowned upon by the passive person as unseemly, undignified or self-serving. Passive people believe that politics is something they want to avoid. As a consequence, they often wind up being manipulated by others who are more dominant. Many creative people who have difficulty in ascending hierarchies substitute idealism of one type or another to gain some sense of superiority that is at least symbolically satisfying to them if not an aid to their upward mobility.

To be sure, there are many creative, assertive and self-assured individuals who do not consciously seek positions of power, who would be quite content with a comparatively status- and duty-free existence. But they are often pushed up into power and leadership positions by more dependent and less self-assured employees who look for someone to whom they can relinquish control and responsibility. Several studies have shown that many of our business and industrial organizations are presently populated by an excessive number of people who show inordinate dependency needs and low-dominance behavior. Psychologist Saul Gellerman feels that dependency today is by far the biggest psychological problem facing business and industry. "It makes people unwilling to take chances, to exert extra effort, to use imagination or to take initiative," says Gellerman, and notes that "dependency is so widespread it seems normal."

Employees who accept a fully dependent status usually erect stiflers and inhibitions that prevent them from trusting their own ideas and judgment in the presence of their superiors. The greater the power gap, the greater will be the dependent person's psychological capitulation.

Psychologist Alfred Adler (in his classic book *Understanding Human Nature*) describes the characteristic attitude of the low-dominance personality as follows:

> People who are permeated by a spirit of servility are likewise not well adapted to positions which demand initiative. They

are comfortable when they are obeying someone else's commands. The servile individual lives by the rules and laws of others, and this type seeks out a servile position almost compulsively. This servile attitude is found in the most varied of life's relationships. One can surmise its existence in the outer carriage, which usually is a somewhat bent and cringing attitude. We see them bending themselves in the presence of others, listening carefully to everyone's words, not so much to weigh and consider them, but rather to carry out their commands, and to echo and reaffirm their sentiments. They consider it an honor to appear submissive, sometimes to a perfectly unbelievable degree.

According to Abraham Maslow, low-dominance feeling implies a lack of self-confidence, a feeling of unworthiness or low ego level. And anthropologist George Maclay emphasizes the almost gravitylike tendency of low-confidence people to seek dependency:

Individuals who have little self-confidence or who have for some special reason lost faith in their ability to run their own lives are more strongly driven to fall into a childlike state of dependence and are eager to exchange self-control for control by an outside authority. Their instinctive ability to defer to a leader develops a hair trigger. They fall into a state of mind which makes them yearn for a powerful ally to whom they can hand over all their responsibilities.

The aggressive person's primary motive is to get as much power as possible to serve his own ends. He sees people as objects and has little feel for them as human beings. He defers to no one. People for him are like chemical compounds with certain characteristics in certain combinations. His narcissism is tempered only by strategic considerations.

Without organizational hierarchies and dominance structures we cannot have productive work. Without power politics we cannot have organizational hierarchies. This state of affairs may be distasteful to many, but it seems to be a fact of life.

5. *One of the most important attributes a supervisor needs to make things work is fairness to subordinates.*

False: Being "fair" means different things to different people, depending on where they are on the submissive-dominance scale. Being "fair" to a submissive, dependent person often means handholding, stroking and other forms of no-pressure handling.

Being "fair" to an aggressive, manipulative person is letting him take over your power and your job. A supervisor must be in command. He must clearly be the person in the pecking order who can peck anyone when he needs to, and who is immune to pecking (or challenges) from subordinates.

A supervisor who cannot do this is seen as weak. His ineffectuality may cause a leadership vacuum which will generate rivalries or resentments among subordinates who want the supervisor's power and think they are more qualified to handle it.

A "fair" boss is often a really wishy-washy boss, like the cartoon character Charlie Brown. Subordinates want a boss who leads, not one who waffles by trying to be "fair" or to be a "nice guy." Being firm, yet courteous and considerate, is the mark of an effective boss. Such a boss is able to generate genuine loyalty and keep hurt feelings to a minimum.

6. *In a fair organization, the most creative persons will succeed and get ahead.*

False: This notion is based on a tunnel vision view of reality. It assumes that an idea's value is crystal clear and can be objectively demonstrated or measured. In actual fact, the value of an idea is what the boss thinks it is in terms of his needs, not according to some objective measure. The performance of a subordinate or the merit of an idea is in the eye of the beholder.

Since bosses must concern themselves with political problems, often the person who is best at solving the boss's difficulties and furthering the boss's ideas will be seen by him as most valuable and deserving of the lion's share of the rewards. Value to the organization is judged by opinion; it is not measured as a scientific fact. It is not an absolute. Creative performance is defined primarily by the needs of the social hierarchy, and secondarily by achievement issues. Often the political issues completely obscure the achievement issues.

One of the chronic problems of performance appraisal systems is that they naively assume objectively measurable performance rather than the reality of politically judged value. There will always be favorites, "fair haired boys" and crown princes. It is human nature.

7. *It is necessary and effective to criticize subordinates for their mistakes.*

True: It is true in the sense that it is necessary to courteously criticize and provide feedback to a person so that learning can take place and the task can be done according to the boss's standards. On the other hand, if criticism is given without courtesy, the person will feel "put down" and become defensive. The resulting emotional upset and stress will reduce his motivation and ability to concentrate on his work. He will often, in retaliation, seek forms of revenge to put the boss "one down" too. At the root of defensiveness is often the fear of losing one's position in the hierarchy by losing face.

If you have ever been chewed out or criticized for an idea, you know how much it stings. The aggressive, power-oriented person knows that harsh criticism is very damaging and he uses it pointedly. The aggressive person lays it on thick because he feels he has the right to make another person feel small or stupid or anxious. The aggressive person usually leaves the person stunned with hurt which evokes the desire to eventually get even, if only indirectly.

The mild-mannered, passive person would seldom be harshly critical of another person's idea. Gossip is the passive person's form of aggression. The passive person would be hard put to confront another person about the merits of his ideas or his performance.

The assertive person is usually reasonably objective in his criticism of ideas and tempers the delivery of the bad news with a courteous and considerate attitude. The assertive person attempts to correct or modify an idea without leaving negative emotions strewn all over the office landscape.

8. *"Packaging" my ideas to get around people's prejudices would be distorting the idea and be a "sellout" of my integrity.*

False: Resistance to new ideas frequently stems from their real or fancied threat to the decision maker's place in the pecking order. A new idea must be "packaged" so that it does not pose any kind of challenge to the position of those who must decide on it.

Individuals at the bottom of the hierarchy often have a more realistic view of the productive value of a new idea because they have less to lose from changes that the new idea might produce in the organizational structure and in people's places in the pecking order. They don't have the "scales of power" covering their eyes. A secretary often sees what the boss misses.

If a new idea or a proposed change is so packaged that it matches the needs of the decision maker, it stands a good chance of acceptance. If, on the other hand, an idea is expected to stand on its own intrinsic merit, it often is doomed to fail. The naive, idealistic notion that ideas and change ought to be judged on their own merits results from unawareness of the pervasive and powerful influences that dominance signaling and hierarchical factors have in decision making.

9. *Being cordial to important people, even if one doesn't like them, is as important as being good at creating new ideas.*

True: Those who manage to achieve a superior position over others exercise their power either consciously or subconsciously. They come to expect at least nominal deference from those who occupy lower positions in the hierarchy.

Yet, a person does not have to "sell out" his ideas by this

deference. Personal integrity and pride can be easily maintained if one is not afraid of articulating one's ideas and principles and has the skills to do so effectively. The sudden growth of the pop psychology movements of Transactional Analysis and Assertiveness Training give testimony to the fact that people perceive these skills to be necessary for promoting their ideas within the confines of an organizational hierarchy.

To become a sophisticated organizational member requires the development of skills to cope with the facts of power without being forced into submissiveness against one's will. Leading an organizational life of "quiet desperation" can be largely avoided by learning assertive techniques. These assuage the sense of helplessness in the face of power, and can turn a purposeless rat race into a compelling challenge and adventure. Nor is it necessary to act like a bear with a toothache to have a reasonable way of life within the organization.

10. *I shouldn't have to curry favor to get people to cooperate with me on my ideas or to do the job they are paid to do.*

False: If you expect someone to do something about your idea because you think they *ought* to do it, you will lead a life of righteous indignation, if not of chronic disappointment. The simple fact is that people will have genuine differences of opinion about what ought to be done about your idea. And even where there is agreement on an idea, people will often disagree on its priority as well as on the way it should be done. One of the measures of the powerful person is his or her ability to persuade people to implement ideas in spite of differing opinions.

To be able to get another person to *want* to do what *you* want them to do is perhaps the most coveted skill in the world of work. It is one of the most effective tools in the kit of the individual who wants to have power over others. It requires close and perceptive observation of people to learn about the things that can serve as incentives for them to further *your* objectives. A kind word, a small favor or a word of praise will often go far in augmenting your influence in the organization.

As you can see, conventional wisdom does little to prepare us for the hard facts of organizational life. It is as though we were raised on a Walt Disney scenario only to find that the real organizational world is more like a Sam Peckinpah script.

Innovation and the implementation of ideas go hand in hand. And just as everyone has the capacity to be creative, so too does every man and woman have the ability to sell ideas through an organizational network. It simply takes initiative, assertiveness and practice.

Always strive for the complete utilization of the entire range of your inventive abilities and above and beyond everything else, just enjoy the challenge of being creative!